IN THE HEART OF
THE COUNTRY

J. M. Coetzee was born in Cape Town, South Africa, in 1940, and educated in South Africa and the United States. His first work of fiction was *Dusklands* (1974), followed by *In the Heart of the Country* (1977), which won the premier South African literary award, the CNA Prize, *Waiting for the Barbarians* (1980), which was awarded the Geoffrey Faber Memorial Prize, the James Tait Black Memorial Prize and the CNA Prize, *Life and Times of Michael K* (1983), which won the Booker Prize and the Prix Etranger Fémina, *Foe* (1986), *Age of Iron* (1990), which won the *Sunday Express* Book of the Year Award. *The Master of Petersburg* (1994), which won the *Irish Times* International Fiction Award and *Disgrace* (1999), which won the Booker Prize, making him the only person to win it twice. J. M. Coetzee was awarded the Jerusalem Prize for 1987. His other works include translations, linguistic studies and literary criticism.

ALSO BY J. M. COETZEE

J. M. Coetzee

IN THE HEART
OF THE COUNTRY

VINTAGE

Published by Vintage 1999

8 1 0 9 7

First published in Great Britain by
Martin Secker & Warburg Limited in 1977

Vintage
Random House, 20 Vauxhall Bridge Road,
London SW1V 2SA

Random House Australia (Pty) Limited
20 Alfred Street, Milsons Point, Sydney
New South Wales 2061, Austalia

Random House New Zealand Limited
18 Poland Road, Glenfield, Auckland 10,
New Zealand

Random House (Pty) Limited
Endulini, 5a Jubilee Road, Parktown 2193,
South Africa

The Random House Group Limited Reg. No. 954009

www.randomhouse.co.uk

A CIP catalogue record for this book
is available from the British Library

ISBN 0 7493 9425 0

Papers used by Random House are natural,
recyclable products made from wood grown in sustain-
able forests. The manufacturing processes conform to the
environmental regulations of the country of origin

Printed and bound in Denmark by
Nørhaven Paperback A/S

1. Today my father brought home his new bride. They came clip-clop across the flats in a dog-cart drawn by a horse with an ostrich-plume waving on its forehead, dusty after the long haul. Or perhaps they were drawn by two plumed donkeys, that is also possible. My father wore his black swallowtail coat and stovepipe hat, his bride a wide-brimmed sunhat and a white dress tight at waist and throat. More detail I cannot give unless I begin to embroider, for I was not watching. I was in my room, in the emerald semi-dark of the shuttered late afternoon, reading a book or, more likely, supine with a damp towel over my eyes fighting a migraine. I am the one who stays in her room reading or writing or fighting migraines. The colonies are full of girls like that, but none, I think, so extreme as I. My father is the one who paces the floorboards back and forth, back and forth in his slow black boots. And then, for a third, there is the new wife, who lies late abed. Those are the antagonists.

2. The new wife. The new wife is a lazy big-boned voluptuous feline woman with a wide slow-smiling mouth. Her eyes are black and shrewd like two berries, two shrewd black berries. She is a big woman with fine wrists and long plump tapering fingers. She eats her food with relish. She sleeps and eats and lazes. She sticks out her long red tongue and licks the sweet mutton-fat from her lips. 'Ah, I like that!' she says, and smiles and rolls her eyes. I watch her mouth mesmerized. Then she turns on me the wide smiling mouth and the shrewd black

eyes. I cannot easily sustain her smile. We are not a happy family together.

3. She is the new wife, therefore the old one is dead. The old wife was my mother, but died so many years ago that I barely recall her. I must have been very young when she died, perhaps only a newborn babe. From one of the farthest oubliettes of memory I extract a faint grey image, the image of a faint grey frail gentle loving mother huddled on the floor, one such as any girl in my position would be likely to make up for herself.

4. My father's first wife, my mother, was a frail gentle loving woman who lived and died under her husband's thumb. Her husband never forgave her for failing to bear him a son. His relentless sexual demands led to her death in childbirth. She was too frail and gentle to give birth to the rough rude boy-heir my father wanted, therefore she died. The doctor came too late. Summoned by a messenger on a bicycle, he had to come trundling along forty miles of farm-track in his donkey-cart. When he arrived my mother already lay composed on her deathbed, patient, bloodless, apologetic.

5. (But why did he not come on horseback? But were there bicycles in those days?)

6. I was not watching my father bear his bride home across the flats because I was in my room in the dark west wing eating my heart out and biding my time. I should have been standing ready to greet them with smiles and offers of tea, but I was not. I was absent. I was not missed. My father pays no attention to my absence. To my father I have been an absence all my life. Therefore instead of being the womanly warmth at the heart of this house I have been a zero, null, a vacuum towards which all collapses inward, a turbulence, muffled, grey, like a chill draft eddying through the corridors, neglected, vengeful.

7. Night falls, and my father and his new wife cavort in the bedroom. Hand in hand they stroke her womb, watching for it to flicker and blossom. They twine; she laps him in her flesh; they chuckle and moan. These are fair times for them.

8. In a house shaped by destiny like an H I have lived all my life, in a theatre of stone and sun fenced in with miles of wire, spinning my trail from room to room, looming over the servants, the grim widow-daughter of the dark father. Sundown after sundown we have faced each other over the mutton, the potatoes, the pumpkin, dull food cooked by dull hands. Is it possible that we spoke? No, we could not have spoken, we must have fronted each other in silence and chewed our way through time, our eyes, his black eyes and my black eyes inherited from him, roaming blank across their fields of vision. Then we have retired to sleep, to dream allegories of baulked desire such as we are blessedly unfitted to interpret; and in the mornings vied in icy asceticism to be the earlier afoot, to lay the fire in the cold grate. Life on the farm.

9. In the shadowy hallway the clock ticks away day and night. I am the one who keeps it wound and who weekly, from sun and almanac, corrects it. Time on the farm is the time of the wide world, neither a jot nor a tittle more or less. Resolutely I beat down the blind, subjective time of the heart, with its spurts of excitement and drags of tedium: my pulse will throb with the steady one-second beat of civilization. One day some as yet unborn scholar will recognize in the clock the machine that has tamed the wilds. But will he ever know the desolation of the hour of the siesta chiming in cool green high-ceilinged houses where the daughters of the colonies lie counting with their eyes shut? The land is full of melancholy spinsters like me, lost to history, blue as roaches in our ancestral homes, keeping a high shine on the copperware and laying in jam. Wooed when we were little by our masterful fathers, we are bitter

3

vestals, spoiled for life. The childhood rape: someone should study the kernel of truth in this fancy.

10. I live, I suffer, I am here. With cunning and treachery, if necessary, I fight against becoming one of the forgotten ones of history. I am a spinster with a locked diary but I am more than that. I am an uneasy consciousness but I am more than that too. When all the lights are out I smile in the dark. My teeth glint, though no one would believe it.

11. She comes up behind me, a waft of orange-blossom and rut, and takes me by the shoulders. 'I do not want you to be angry, I understand that you should feel disturbed and unhappy, but there is no cause for it. I would like us all to be happy together. I will do anything, truly anything, to make that come about. Can you believe me?'

I stare into the chimney-recess; my nose swells and reddens.

'I want to make a happy household,' she croons, circling, 'the three of us together. I want you to think of me as a sister, not an enemy.'

I watch the full lips of this glutted woman.

12. There was a time when I imagined that if I talked long enough it would be revealed to me what it means to be an angry spinster in the heart of nowhere. But though I sniff at each anecdote like a dog at its doo, I find none of that heady expansion into the as-if that marks the beginning of a true double life. Aching to form the words that will translate me into the land of myth and hero, here I am still my dowdy self in a dull summer heat that will not transcend itself. What do I lack? I weep and gnash my teeth. Is it mere passion? Is it merely a vision of a second existence passionate enough to carry me from the mundane of being into the doubleness of signification? Do I not quiver at every pore with a passion of vexation? Is it that my passion lacks will? Am I an angry yet somehow after all complacent farmyard spinster, wrapped in the embrace of

my furies? Do I truly wish to get beyond myself? The story of my rage and its dire sequel: am I going to climb into this vehicle and close my eyes and be carried downstream over the rapids, through the broken water, to wake refreshed on the quiet estuary? What automatism is this, what liberation is it going to bring me, and without liberation what is the point of my story? Do I feel rich outrage at my spinster fate? Who is behind my oppression? You and you, I say, crouching in the cinders, stabbing my finger at father and stepmother. But why have I not run away from them? As long as an elsewhere exists where I can lead a life, there are heavenly fingers pointing at me too. Or am I, hitherto unbeknown to me, but now alas known, reserved for a more complex fate: to be crucified head downward as a warning to those who love their rage and lack all vision of another tale? But what other tale is there for me? Marriage to the neighbour's second son? I am not a happy peasant. I am a miserable black virgin, and my story is my story, even if it is a dull black blind stupid miserable story, ignorant of its meaning and of all its many possible untapped happy variants. I am I. Character is fate. History is God. Pique, pique, pique.

13. The Angel, that is how she is sometimes known, The Angel in Black who comes to save the children of the brown folk from their croups and fevers. All her household severity is transformed into an unremitting compassion when it comes to the care of the sick. Night after night she sits up with whimpering children or women in labour, fighting off sleep. 'An angel from heaven!' they say, their flatterers' eyes keen. Her heart sings. In war she would lighten the last hours of the wounded. They would die with smiles on their lips, gazing into her eyes, clasping her hand. Her stores of compassion are boundless. She needs to be needed. With no one to need her she is baffled and bewildered. Does that not explain everything?

14. If my father had been a weaker man he would have had a

better daughter. But he has never needed anything. Enthralled by my need to be needed, I circle him like a moon. Such is my sole risible venture into the psychology of our débâcle. To explain is to forgive, to be explained is to be forgiven, but I, I hope and fear, am inexplicable, unforgivable. (Yet what is it in me that shrinks from the light? Do I really have a secret or is this bafflement before myself only a way of mystifying my better, questing half? Do I truly believe that stuffed in a crack between my soft mother and my baby self lies the key to this black bored spinster? Prolong yourself, prolong yourself, that is the whisper I hear in my inmost.)

15. Another aspect of myself, now that I am talking about myself, is my love of nature, particularly of insect life, of the scurrying purposeful life that goes on around each ball of dung and under every stone. When I was a little girl (weave, weave!) in a frilled sunbonnet I would sit all day in the dust, so the story goes, playing with my friends the beetles, the grey ones and the brown ones and the big black ones whose names I forget but could with no effort turn up in an encyclopedia, and my friends the anteaters who made those elegant little conical sandtraps down whose sides I would tumble the common red ant, and, every now and again, secreted beneath a flat stone, a pale dazed flaccid baby scorpion, whom I would crush with a stick, for even then I knew that scorpions were bad. I have no fear of insects. I leave the homestead behind and walk barefoot up the river bed, the hot dark sand crunching beneath my soles and squeezing out between my toes. In the drifts I sit with spread skirts feeling the warmth mould itself to my thighs. I would have no qualm, I am sure, if it came to the pinch, though how it could come to this pinch I do not know, about living in a mud hut, or indeed under a lean-to of branches, out in the veld, eating chickenfeed, talking to the insects. Even through the little girl the lineaments of the crazy old lady must have glimmered, and the brown folk, who hide behind bushes and know everything, must have chuckled.

16. I grew up with the servants' children. I spoke like one of them before I learned to speak like this. I played their stick and stone games before I knew I could have a dolls' house with Father and Mother and Peter and Jane asleep in their own beds and clean clothes ready in the chest whose drawers slid in and out while Nan the dog and Felix the cat snoozed before the kitchen coals. With the servants' children I searched the veld for khamma-roots, fed cowsmilk to the orphaned lambs, hung over the gate to watch the sheep dipped and the Christmas pig shot. I smelled the sour recesses where they slept pell-mell like rabbits, I sat at the feet of their blind old grandfather while he whittled clothes-pegs and told his stories of bygone days when men and beasts migrated from winter grazing to summer grazing and lived together on the trail. At the feet of an old man I have drunk in a myth of a past when beast and man and master lived a common life as innocent as the stars in the sky, and I am far from laughing. How am I to endure the ache of whatever it is that is lost without a dream of a pristine age, tinged perhaps with the violet of melancholy, and a myth of expulsion to interpret my ache to me? And mother, soft scented loving mother who drugged me with milk and slumber in the featherbed and then, to the sound of bells in the night, vanished, leaving me alone among rough hands and hard bodies – where are you? My lost world is a world of men, of cold nights, woodfire, gleaming eyes, and a long tale of dead heroes in a language I have not unlearned.

17. In this house with rival mistresses the servants go about their duties with hunched shoulders, flinching from the dregs of bad temper that will be flung at them. Bored with drudgery, they look forward to the colour and drama of quarrels, though they know that few things are better for them than amity. The day has not yet come when the giants war among themselves and the dwarves slip away in the night. Feeling all their feelings not successively in waves of contraries but simultaneously as a hotchpotch of rage, regret, resentment, and

7

glee, they experience a giddiness that makes them long to be asleep. They want to be in the big house but they also want to stay at home malingering, dozing on a bench in the shade. Cups fall through their fingers and shatter on the floor. They whisper rapidly in corners. For no good reason they scold their children. They have bad dreams. The psychology of servants.

18. I live neither alone nor in society but as it were among children. I am spoken to not in words, which come to me quaint and veiled, but in signs, in conformations of face and hands, in postures of shoulders and feet, in nuances of tune and tone, in gaps and absences whose grammar has never been recorded. Reading the brown folk I grope, as they grope reading me: for they too hear my words only dully, listening for those overtones of the voice, those subtleties of the eyebrows that tell them my true meaning 'Beware, do not cross me,' 'What I say does not come from me.' Across valleys of space and time we strain ourselves to catch the pale smoke of each other's signals. That is why my words are not words such as men use to men. Alone in my room with my duties behind me and the lamp steadily burning I creak into rhythms that are my own, stumble over the rocks of words that I have never heard on another tongue. I create myself in the words that create me, I who living among the downcast have never beheld myself in the equal regard of another's eye, have never held another in the equal regard of mine. While I am free to be I, nothing is impossible. In the cloister of my room I am the mad hag I am destined to be. My clothes cake with dribble, I hunch and twist, my feet blossom with horny callouses, this prim voice, spinning out sentences without occasion, gaping with boredom because nothing ever happens on the farm, cracks and oozes the peevish loony sentiments that belong to the dead of night when the censor snores, to the crazy hornpipe I dance with myself.

19. What solace are lapidary paradoxes for the loves of the

body? I watch the full lips of the glutted widow, hear the creak of floorboards in the muted farmhouse, the warm murmur from the great bed, feel the balm of loving flesh upon me, sleep away into the steaming body smells. But how to let go the real for the deep darkdown desired? A jagged virgin, I stand in the doorway, naked, asking.

20. To her full dark lips the glutted widow raises a finger in cryptic gesture. Does she warn me to silence? Does my candid body amuse her? Through the open curtains stream the rays of the full moon on to her shoulders, her full ironical lips. In the shadow of her haunch lies the man asleep. To her mouth she raises a cryptic hand. Is she amused? Is she startled? The night breeze wafts through the parted curtains. The room is in darkness, the sleeping figures so still I cannot hear their breathing above the hammer of my heart. Should I go to them clothed? Are they phantoms who will vanish when I touch them? She watches me with full ironical lips. I drop my clothes at the door. In the glare of the moonlight she goes over my poor beseeching body. I weep, hiding my eyes, wishing for a life story that will wash over me tranquilly as it does for other women.

21. When he came in hot and dusty after a day's work my father expected that his bath should be ready for him. It was my childhood duty to light the fire an hour before sunset so that the hot water could be poured into the enamelled hipbath the moment he stamped through the front door. Then I would retire to the dark side of the floral screen to receive his clothes and lay out the clean underlinen. Tiptoeing out of the bathroom I would hear the wash of his entry, the sucking of the water under his armpits and between his buttocks, and inhale the sweet damp heavy miasma of soap and sweat. Later this duty ceased; but when I think of male flesh, white, heavy, dumb, whose flesh can it be but his?

22. Through a chink in the curtain I watch them. Taking his hand, lifting her skirt, she steps down, one-two, from the dog-cart. She stretches her arms, smiling, yawning, a little parasol dangling closed from a gloved finger. He stands behind her. Low words pass. They come up the steps. Her eyes are full and happy, the kind of eyes that do not notice fingers at the lace curtains. Her legs swing easily, at peace with her body. They pass through the door and out of sight, sauntering, a man and a woman come home.

23. Into the evening, as the shadows first lengthen and then cover everything, I stand at the window. Hendrik crosses the yard on his way to the storeroom. The massed twitter of birds in the riverbed rises and wanes. In the last light the swallows swoop to their nest under the eaves and the first bats flit out. From their various lairs the predators emerge, *muishond, meerkat.* What are pain, jealousy, loneliness doing in the African night? Does a woman looking through a window into the dark mean anything? I place all ten fingertips on the cool glass. The wound in my chest slides open. If I am an emblem then I am an emblem. I am incomplete, I am a being with a hole inside me, I signify something, I do not know what, I am dumb, I stare out through a sheet of glass into a darkness that is complete, that lives in itself, bats, bushes, predators and all, that does not regard me, that is blind, that does not signify but merely is. If I press harder the glass will break, blood will drip, the cricket-song will stop for a moment and then resume. I live inside a skin inside a house. There is no act I know of that will liberate me into the world. There is no act I know of that will bring the world into me. I am a torrent of sound streaming into the universe, thousands upon thousands of corpuscles weeping, groaning, gnashing their teeth.

24. They sweat and strain, the farmhouse creaks through the night. Already the seed must have been planted, soon she will be sprawling about in her mindless heat, swelling and ripening,

waiting for her little pink pig to knock. Whereas a child I bore, assuming that such a calamity could ever befall me, would be thin and sallow, would weep without cease from aches in his vitals, would totter from room to room on his rickety pins clutching at his mother's apron-strings and hiding his face from strangers. But who would give me a baby, who would not turn to ice at the spectacle of my bony frame on the wedding-couch, the coat of fur up to my navel, the acrid cavities of my armpits, the line of black moustache, the eyes, watchful, defensive, of a woman who has never lost possession of herself? What huffing and puffing there would have to be before my house could be blown down! Who could wake my slumbering eggs? And who would attend my childbed? My father, scowling, with a whip? The brown folk, cowed servitors, kneeling to offer a trussed lamb, first fruits, wild honey, sniggering at the miracle of the virgin birth? Out of his hole he pokes his snout, son of the father, Antichrist of the desert come to lead his dancing hordes to the promised land. They whirl and beat drums, they shake axes and pitchforks they follow the babe, while in the kitchen his mother conjures over the fire, or tears out the guts of cocks, or cackles in her bloody armchair. A mind mad enough for parricide and pseudo-matricide and who knows what other atrocities can surely encompass an epileptic Führer and the march of a band of overweening serfs on a country town from whose silver roofs the sunfire winks and from whose windows they are idly shot to pieces. They lie in the dust, sons and daughters of the Hottentots, flies crawl in their wounds, they are carted off and buried in a heap. Labouring under my father's weight I struggle to give life to a world but seem to engender only death.

25. By the light of a storm-lantern I see that they sleep the sleep of the blissfully sated, she on her back, her nightdress rucked about her hips, he face down, his left hand folded in hers. I bring not the meat-cleaver as I thought it would be but

the hatchet, weapon of the Valkyries. I deepen myself in the stillness like a true lover of poetry, breathing with their breath.

26. My father lies on his back, naked, the fingers of his right hand twined in the fingers of her left, the jaw slack, the dark eyes closed on all their fire and lightning, a liquid rattle coming from the throat, the tired blind fish, cause of all my woe, lolling in his groin (would that it had been dragged out long ago with all its roots and bulbs!). The axe sweeps up over my shoulder. All kinds of people have done this before me, wives, sons, lovers, heirs, rivals, I am not alone. Like a ball on a string it floats down at the end of my arm, sinks into the throat below me, and all is suddenly tumult. The woman snaps upright in bed, glaring about her, drenched in blood, bewildered by the angry wheezing and spouting at her side. How fortunate that at times like these the larger action flows of itself and requires of the presiding figure no more than presence of mind! She wriggles her nightdress decently over her hips. Leaning forward and gripping what must be one of their four knees, I deliver much the better chop deep into the crown of her head. She dips over into the cradle of her lap and topples leftward in a ball, my dramatic tomahawk still embedded in her. (Who would have thought I had such strokes in me?) But fingers are scratching at me from this side of the bed, I am off balance, I must keep a cool head, I must pick them off one by one, recover (with some effort) my axe, and hack with distaste at these hands, these arms until I have a free moment to draw a sheet over all this shuddering and pound it into quiet. Here I am beating with a steady rhythm, longer perhaps than is necessary, but calming myself too in preparation for what must be a whole new phase of my life. For no longer need I fret about how to fill my days. I have broken a commandment, and the guilty cannot be bored. I have two fullgrown bodies to get rid of besides many other traces of my violence. I have a face to compose, a story to invent, and all before dawn when Hendrik comes for the milking-pail!

27. I ask myself: Why, since the moment she came clip-clop across the flats in the dog-cart drawn by a horse with ostrich-plumes in its harness, dusty after the long haul, in her wide-brimmed hat, have I refused speech with her, stubbornly exerting myself to preserve the monologue of my life? Can I imagine what it would have been like to turn the pages of the mornings with her over steaming teacups, with the chickens clucking outside and the servants chattering softly in the kitchen, in whatever spirit, guarded or peaceful? Can I imagine cutting out patterns with her, or strolling through the orchard hand in hand, giggling? Is it possible that I am a prisoner not of the lonely farmhouse and the stone desert but of my stony monologue? Have my blows been aimed at shutting those knowing eyes or at silencing her voice? Might we not, bent over our teacups, have learned to coo to each other, or, drifting past each other in the dark corridor, hot and sleepless in the siesta hour, have touched, embraced, and clung? Might those mocking eyes not have softened, might I not have yielded, might we not have lain in each other's arms all afternoon whispering, two girls together? I stroke her forehead, she nuzzles my hand, I am held in the dark pools of her eyes, I do not mind.

28. I ask myself: What is it in me that lures me into forbidden bedrooms and makes me commit forbidden acts? Has a lifetime in the desert, wrapped in this funnel of black cloth, wound me into such a coil of vicious energy that the merest pedlar or visiting third cousin would find himself poisoned at his meat or hatcheted in bed? Does an elementary life burn people down to elementary states, to pure anger, pure gluttony, pure sloth? Am I unfitted by my upbringing for a life of more complex feelings? Is that why I have never left the farm, foreign to townslife, preferring to immerse myself in a landscape of symbol where simple passions can spin and fume around their own centres, in limitless space, in endless time, working out their own forms of damnation?

13

29. I ask myself: But am I doing justice to the city? Is it not possible to conceive a city above whose rooftops drift the wisps of a thousand private fires, from whose streets rises the susurrus of a thousand pattering damned voices? Perhaps; but it is too painterly, and I am not a painter.

30. I ask myself: What am I going to do with the bodies?

31. Far down in the earth flow the underground rivers, through dark caverns dripping with crystalline water, graves, if only they could be reached, for all the family secrets in the world. I wade out into the tepid dam looking for the sinkhole which in our dreams beckons from the deep and leads to the underground kingdom. My skirt billows and floats around my waist like a black flower. My feet are soothed by the red slime, the green duckweed. Like abandoned twins my shoes watch from the bank. Of all adventures suicide is the most literary, more so even than murder. With the story coming to its end, all one's last bad poetry finds release. I cast a long calm look of farewell at the sky and the stars, which probably cast a long calm vacant look back, exhale the last beloved breath (goodbye, spirit!), and dive for the abyss. Then the elegiac trance passes and all the rest is cold, wet, and farcical. My underwear balloons with water. I strike bottom all too soon, as far from the mythic vortex as ever. The first willed draught of water through my nostrils sets off a cough and the blind panic of an organism that wants to live. I haul myself to the surface with legs and arms. My head breaks gasping and retching into the night air. I try to launch myself into the horizontal but I am weary, weary. Perhaps I strike out once or twice with wooden arms. Perhaps I sink a second time, tasting the water with less revulsion now. Perhaps I come to the surface again, still thrashing, but also waiting for an interlude of stillness to test and taste the languor of my muscles. Perhaps I beat the water now in one spot only, making a last bargain, giving up a breath for the sake of a single word, half water, half plea to the absent, to all the absent, who

congregate now in the sky in a whirlwind of absence, removed, sightless, to call off the dogs, to call off the joke, before I sink again and turn myself to the serious exploration of my last moments.

32. But what do I know about exploring these deeps, I, a drudgemaiden who has spent her days over a cooking-pot in a sooty corner and her nights pressing her knuckles into her eyes, watching the rings of light cascade and spin, waiting for visions? Like killing, dying is probably a story drearier than the one I tell myself. Deprived of human intercourse, I inevitably overvalue the imagination and expect it to make the mundane glow with an aura of self-transcendence. Yet why these glorious sunsets, I ask myself, if nature does not speak to us with tongues of fire? (I am unconvinced by talk about suspended dust particles.) Why crickets all night long and birdsong at dawn? But it is late. If there is a time for rumination there is also a time to go back to the kitchen, and at this moment I have a serious matter to attend to, the disposal of the corpses. For soon Hendrik is going to open the back door, and while it is true that the essence of servanthood is the servant's intimacy with his master's dirt, and while it is also true that there is a perspective in which corpses are dirt, Hendrik is not only essence but substance, not only servant but stranger. First Hendrik will come for the milking-pail, then, a little later, Anna, to wash the dishes, sweep the floor, make the beds. What will Anna think when she finds the household still but for the steady sound of scrubbing from the master's bedroom? She hesitates, listening, before she knocks. I cry out in fright, she hears me muffled through the heavy door: 'No, not today! Anna, is that you? Not today – come back tomorrow. Now go away, please.' She pads off. Standing with an ear to the crack I hear the back door close behind her, then, though she ought to be out of earshot, the trot of her feet on the gravel. Has she smelled blood? Has she gone to tell?

33. The woman lies on her side with her knees drawn up to her chin. If I do not hurry she will set in that position. Her hair falls over her face in a sticky dark-red wing. Though her last act was to flinch from the terrific axe, screwing her eyes shut, clenching her teeth, the face has now relaxed. But the man, tenacious of life, has moved. His final experience must have been an unsatisfactory one, a groping with dulled muscles toward an illusory zone of safety. He lies head and arms over the edge of the bed, black with his heavy blood. It would have been better for him to have yielded the gentle ghost, following it as far as he could on its passage out, closing his eyes on the image of a swallow swooping, rising, riding.

34. How fortunate at times like these that there is only one problem, a problem of cleanliness. Until this bloody afterbirth is gone there can be no new life for me. The bedclothes are soaked and will have to be burned. The mattress too will have to be burned, though not today. There is a quag of blood on the floor and there will be more blood when I shift the bodies. What of the bodies? They can be burned or buried or submerged. If buried or submerged they will have to leave the house. If buried they can be buried only where the earth is soft, in the riverbed. But if buried in the riverbed they will be washed out in the next spate, or in the one after that, and return to the world lolling in each other's rotten arms against the fence where the fence crosses the river. If weighted and sunk in the dam, they will contaminate the water and reappear as chained skeletons grinning to the sky in the next drought. But buried or drowned, they will have to be shifted, whether entire in barrowloads or in parcels. How clearly my mind works, like the mind of a machine. Am I strong enough to move them unaided in a wheelbarrow, or must I hack away until I have portable sections? Am I equal to carrying even a single mono-lithic trunk? Is there a way of partitioning a trunk without obscenity? I should have paid more attention to the art of butchery. And how does one chain flesh to rock without drilling

holes? And with what? An auger? A brace and bit? What of exposure on an antheap as an alternative, or exposure on a remote part of the farm, in a cave? What of a funeral pyre in the back yard? What of firing the house about all our ears? Am I equal to that?

35. Of course the truth is that I am equal to anything. I am nothing if not embarrassed by my freedom, these tasks require only patience and meticulousness, of which, like the ant, I have overmuch, besides a steady stomach. If I go wandering in the hills I am sure that, in time, I will find boulders with holes through them, worn by the dripping of water in a bygone ice age, no doubt, or forged in a volcanic cataclysm. In the wagonhouse there are bound to be yards of providential chain, hitherto invisible, now suddenly leaping into sight, and casks of gunpowder, faggots of sandalwood. But what I now find myself wondering is whether it is not time for me to find a strong-thewed accomplice who, without pause for question, will swing the corpses on to his shoulders and stride off to dispose of them in some swift, effective way, such as stuffing them down an exhausted borehole and capping it with a mighty rock. For the day will come when I must have another human being, must hear another voice, even if it speaks only abuse. This monologue of the self is a maze of words out of which I shall not find a way until someone else gives me a lead. I roll my eyeballs, I pucker my lips, I stretch my ears, but the face in the mirror is my face and will go on being mine even if I hold it in the fire till it drips. No matter with what frenzy I live the business of death or wallow in blood and soapsuds, no matter what wolf howls I hurl into the night, my acts, played out within the macabre theatre of myself, remain mere behaviour. I offend no one, for there is no one to offend but the servants and the dead. How shall I be saved? And can this really be I (scrub-scrub-scrub), this bare-kneed lady? Have I, the true deepdown I beyond words, participated in these phenomena any more deeply than by simply being present at a moment in

17

time, a point in space, at which a block of violence, followed by a block of scrubbing, for the sake of the servants, rattled past on their way from nowhere to nowhere? If I turn my back and walk away will this whole bloody lamplit scene not dwindle down the tunnel of memory, pass through the gates of horn, and leave me grinding my knuckles in my eyes in the grim little room at the end of the passage, waiting for my father's eyebrows to coalesce, then the black pools beneath them, then the cavern of the mouth from which echoes and echoes his eternal NO?

36. For he does not die so easily after all. Disgruntled, saddle-sore, it is he who rides in out of the sunset, who nods when I greet him, who stalks into the house and slumps in his armchair waiting for me to help him off with his boots. The old days are not gone after all. He has not brought home a new wife, I am still his daughter, if I can unsay the bad words perhaps even his good daughter, though it would be well, I can see, to keep out of his way while he ruminates a failure which I, innocent of the ways of courtship, kept all my life in the economic dark, will fail to understand. My heart leaps at this second chance, but I move demurely, I bow my head.

37. My father pushes his food aside untouched. He sits in the front room staring into the grate. I light a lamp for him, but he waves me away. In my room I pick at a hem and tune my ears to his silence. Does he sigh between the chimes of the clock? I undress and sleep. In the morning the front room is empty.

38. Six months ago Hendrik brought home his new bride. They came clip-clop across the flats in the donkey-cart, dusty after the long haul from Armoede. Hendrik wore the black suit passed on to him by my father with an old wide-brimmed felt hat and a shirt buttoned to the throat. His bride sat by his side clutching her shawl, exposed and apprehensive. Hendrik had

bought her from her father for six goats and a five-pound note, with a promise of five pounds more, or perhaps of five goats more, one does not always hear these things well. I have never seen Armoede, I seem never to have been anywhere, I seem to know nothing for sure, perhaps I am simply a ghost or a vapour floating at the intersection of a certain latitude and a certain longitude, suspended here by an unimaginable tribunal until a certain act is committed, a stake is driven through the heart of a corpse buried at a crossroads, perhaps, or somewhere a castle crumbles into a tarn, whatever that may be. I have never been to Armoede, but with no effort at all, this is one of my faculties, I can bring to life the bleak windswept hill, the iron shanties with hessian in the doorways, the chickens, doomed, scratching in the dust, the cold snot-nosed children toiling back from the dam with buckets of water, the same chickens scattering now before the donkey-cart in which Hendrik bears away his child-bride, bashful, kerchiefed, while the six dowry-goats nuzzle the thorns and watch through their yellow eyes a scene in its plenitude forever unknowable to me, the thorn-bushes, the midden, the chickens, the children scampering behind the cart, all held in a unity under the sun, innocent, but to me only names, names, names. There is no doubt about it, what keeps me going (see the tears roll down the slopes of my nose, only metaphysics keeps them from falling on the page, I weep for that lost innocence, mine and mankind's) is my determination, my iron determination, my iron intractable risible determination to burst through the screen of names into the goatseye view of Armoede and the stone desert, to name only these, in despite of all the philosophers have said (and what do I, poor provincial blackstocking, know about philosophy, as the lamp gutters and the clock strikes ten?).

39. Locked in sleep she lies all night at Hendrik's side, a child still growing, now a fraction at the knee, now a fraction at the wrist, the proportions always suave. In the old days, the bygone days when Hendrik and his kin followed their fat-tailed sheep

from pasture to pasture, the golden age before the worm arrived, on the wings of the howling storm no doubt, and decamped at the very spot where I sit, what a coincidence, perhaps then, when Hendrik was a patriarch bowing his knee to no one, he took to bed two wives who revered him, did his will, adapted their bodies to his desires, slept tight against him, the old wife on one side, the young wife on the other, that is how I imagine it. But tonight Hendrik has only one wife, and old Jakob in the schoolhouse has only one wife, who pouts and mutters. Borne on the wind at nightfall comes her crosspatch voice, the words blessedly indistinct, one cannot have too little of quarrelling, but the tunes of denunciation quite clear.

40. This is not Hendrik's home. No one is ancestral to the stone desert, no one but the insects, among whom myself a thin black beetle with dummy wings who lays no eggs and blinks in the sun, a real puzzle to entomology. Hendrik's forebears in the olden days crisscrossed the desert with their flocks and their chattels, heading from A to B or from X to Y, sniffing for water, abandoning stragglers, making forced marches. Then one day fences began to go up – I speculate of course – men on horseback rode up and from shadowed faces issued invitations to stop and settle that might also have been orders and might have been threats, one does not know, and so one became a herdsman, and one's children after one, and one's women took in washing. Fascinating, this colonial history: I wonder whether a speculative history is possible, as a speculative philosophy, a speculative theology, and now, it would appear, a speculative entomology are possible, all sucked out of my thumb, to say nothing of the geography of the stone desert and animal husbandry. And economics: how am I to explain the economics of my existence, with its migraines and siestas, its ennui, its speculative languors, unless the sheep have something to eat (for this is not finally an insect farm); and what have I provided for them but stone and scrub? It must be the scrub that nourishes the sheep that nourish me, the bleached scrubgrass, the

grey scrub-bushes, dreary to my eye but bursting with virtue and succulence to the sheep's. There is another great moment in colonial history: the first merino is lifted from shipboard, with block and tackle, in a canvas waistband, bleating with terror, unaware that this is the promised land where it will browse generation after generation on the nutritious scrub and provide the economic base for the presence of my father and myself in this lonely house where we kick our heels waiting for the wool to grow and gather about ourselves the remnants of the lost tribes of the Hottentots to be hewers of wood and drawers of water and shepherds and body-servants in perpetuity and where we are devoured by boredom and pull the wings off flies.

41. Hendrik was not born here. He arrived from nowhere, the child of some father and some mother unknown to me, sent into the world in hard times, with or without a blessing, to earn his bread. He arrived one afternoon asking for work, though why here I cannot imagine, we are on the road from no A to no B in the world, if such a fate is topologically possible, I hope I use the word correctly, I have never had a tutor, I am not one of those long-legged hoydens that wandering tutors love to draw a stool up next to, but dour and sweaty and stupid with anxiety. Hendrik arrived one afternoon, a boy of sixteen, I am guessing, dusty of course, with a stick in his hand and a bag on his shoulder, stopping at the foot of the steps and looking up to where my father sat smoking and staring into the distance: that is our wont here, that must be the origin of our speculative bias, staring into the distance, staring into the fire. Hendrik doffed his hat, a characteristic gesture, a sixteen-year-old boy holding his hat to his breast, men and boys all wear hats here.

'Baas,' said Hendrik, 'good day, baas. I am looking for work.'

My father hawked and swallowed. I render his words; I cannot know whether Hendrik heard what I heard besides, what I perhaps did not hear that day but hear now in my inner ear, the penumbra of moodishness or disdain about the words.

'What kind of work are you looking for?'

'Anything – just work, baas.'

'Where are you from?'

'From Armoede, my baas. But now I come from baas Kobus. Baas Kobus says the baas has work here.'

'Do you work for baas Kobus?'

'No, I do not work for baas Kobus. I was there looking for work. Then baas Kobus said that the baas has work. So I came.'

'What kind of work can you do? Can you work with sheep?'

'Yes, I know sheep, baas.'

'How old are you? Can you count?'

'I am strong. I will work. The baas will see.'

'Are you by yourself?'

'Yes baas, I am by myself now.'

'Do you know the people on my farm?'

'No baas, I know no one around here.'

'Now listen carefully. What is your name?'

'Hendrik, my baas.'

'Listen carefully, Hendrik. Go to the kitchen and tell Anna to give you bread and coffee. Tell her she must fix a place for you to sleep. Tomorrow morning early I want you here. Then I will tell you your job. Now go.'

'Yes, my baas. Thank you, my baas.'

42. How satisfying, the flow of this dialogue. Would that all my life were like that, question and answer, word and echo, instead of the torment of And next? And next? Men's talk is so unruffled, so serene, so full of common purpose. I should have been a man, I would not have grown up so sour, I would have spent my days in the sun doing whatever it is that men do, digging holes, building fences, counting sheep. What is there for me in the kitchen? The patter of maids, gossip, ailments, babies, steam, foodsmells, catfur at the ankles – what kind of life can I make of these? Even decades of mutton and

pumpkin and potatoes have failed to coax from me the jowls, the bust, the hips of a true country foodwife, have achieved no more than to send my meagre buttocks sagging down the backs of my legs. For alas, the power of my will, which I picture to myself as wire sheathed in crêpe, has not after all been great enough to keep me forever pristine against those molecules of fat: perishing by the million in their campaigns against the animalcules of my blood, they yet push their way forward, a tide of blind mouths, that is how I imagine it, as I sit year after year across the table from my silent father, listening to the tiny teeth inside me. One should not expect miracles from a body. Even I will die. How chastening.

43. The mirror. Inherited from my long-lost mother, whose portrait it must be that hangs on the wall of the dining-room over the heads of my silent father and my silent self, though why it is that when I conjure up that wall I find below the picture-rail only a grey blur, a strip of grey blur, if such is imaginable, traced out by my eye along the wall . . . Inherited from my long-lost mother, whom one day I shall find, the mirror fills the door of the wardrobe opposite my bed. It gives me no pleasure to pore over reflections of my body, but when I have sheathed myself in my nightgown, which is white – white for nighttime, black for daytime, that is how I dress – and my bedsocks for the winter cold and my nightcap for the drafts, I sometimes leave the light burning and recline abed sustained on my elbow and smile at the image that reclines abed facing me sustained on an elbow, and sometimes even talk to it, or her. It is at times like these that I notice (what a helpful device a mirror is for bringing things into the open, if one can call it a device, so simple is it, so devoid of mechanism) how thickly the hair grows between my eyes, and wonder whether my glower, my rodent glower, to mince no words, I have no cause to love this face, might not be cosmetically tempered if I plucked out some of that hair with tweezers, or even all of it in a bunch, like carrots, with a pair of pliers, thereby pushing

23

my eyes apart and creating an illusion of grace and even temper.
And might I not soften my aspect too if I released my hair from
its daytime net and pins, its nighttime cap, and washed it, and
let it fall first to the nape of my neck, then perhaps one day to
my shoulders, if it grows for corpses why should it not grow
for me? And might I not be less ugly if I did something about
my teeth, of which I have too many, by sacrificing some to
give the others space to grow in, if I am not too old for growth?
How equably I contemplate pulling out teeth: many things I
fear but pain does not seem to be one of them. I would seat
myself (I say to myself) in front of the mirror, clench the jaws
of the pliers on a condemned tooth, and tug and worry till it
came out. Then I would go on to the next one. And having
done the teeth and the eyebrows I would go on to the com-
plexion. I would run down to the orchard every morning and
stand under the trees, the apricot-trees, the peach-trees, the
fig-trees, devouring fruit until my bowels relented. I would take
exercise, a morning walk down the riverbed, an evening walk
on the hillside. If the cause be physical that makes my skin so
dull and pallid, my flesh so thin and heavy, if such combinations
are possible, that I sometimes wonder whether the blood flows
in me or merely stands in pools, or whether I have twenty-one
skins instead of seven, as the books say – if the cause be physical
then the cure must be physical; if not, what is there left to
believe in?

44. But what a joy it would be to be merely plain, to be a
plain placid empty-headed heiress anxious not to be left on the
shelf, ready to commit herself body and soul to the first willing
fellow to pass by, a pedlar even, or an itinerant teacher of Latin,
and breed him six daughters, and bear his blows and curses
with Christian fortitude, and live a decent obscure life instead
of leaning on an elbow watching myself in the mirror in an
atmosphere of gathering gloom and doom, if my bones tell me
aright. Why, when I am able so relentlessly to leave my warm
bed at five in the morning to light the stove, my feet blue with

cold, my fingers cleaving to the frozen ironware, can I not leap up now, run through the moonlight to the toolchest, to the orchard, and begin the whole regimen of hair-plucking and tooth-pulling and fruit-eating before it is too late? Is there something in me that loves the gloomy, the hideous, the doom-ridden, that sniffs out its nest and snuggles down in a dark corner among rats' droppings and chicken-bones rather than resign itself to decency? And if there is, where does it come from? From the monotony of my surroundings? From all these years in the heart of nature, seven leagues from the nearest neighbour, playing with sticks and stones and insects? I think not, though who am I to say. From my parents? From my father, angry, loveless? From my mother, that blurred oval behind my father's head? Perhaps. Perhaps from them, jointly and severally, and behind them from my four grandparents, whom I have forgotten but could certainly recall in case of need, and my eight great-grandparents and my sixteen great-great-grand-parents, unless there is incest in the line, and the thirty-two before them and so forth until we come to Adam and Eve and finally to the hand of God, by a process whose mathematics has always eluded me. Original sin, degeneracy of the line: there are two fine, bold hypotheses for my ugly face and my dark desires, and for my disinclination to leap out of bed this instant and cure myself. But explanations do not interest me. I am beyond the why and wherefore of myself. Fate is what I am interested in; or, failing fate, whatever it is that is going to happen to me. The woman in the nightcap watching me from the mirror, the woman who in a certain sense is me, will dwindle and expire here in the heart of the country unless she has at least a thin porridge of event to live on. I am not interested in becoming one of those people who look into mirrors and see nothing, or walk in the sun and cast no shadow. It is up to me.

45. Hendrik. Hendrik is paid in kind and cash. What was once two shillings at the end of the month has now grown to six

shillings. Also two slaughter-sheep and weekly rations of flour, mealie-meal, sugar, and coffee. He has his own vegetable patch. He is clothed in my father's good castoffs. He makes shoes for himself from skins that he cures and tans. His Sundays are his own. In sickness he is cared for. When he grows too old to work his duties will be passed on to a younger man and he will retire to a bench in the sun from where he will watch his grandchildren at their play. His grave is marked out for him in the graveyard. His daughters will close his eyes. There are other ways of arranging things, but none that I know of so pacific as this.

46. Hendrik wishes to start a line, a humble line of his own in parallel to the line of my grandfather and my father, to speak only of them. Hendrik would like a house full of sons and daughters. That is why he has married. The second son, he thinks, the obedient one, will stay behind, learn the farmwork, be a pillar of help, marry a good girl, and continue the line. The daughters, he thinks, will work in the farmhouse kitchen. On Saturday nights they will be courted by boys from the neighbouring farms, come epic distances across the veld on their bicycles with guitars strapped on their shoulders, and bear children out of wedlock. The first son, the quarrelsome one, the one who will not say Yes, will leave home to find work on the railways, and be stabbed in a brawl, and die alone, and break his mother's heart. As for the other sons, the obscure ones, perhaps they too will leave in search of work and never be heard of again, or perhaps they will die in infancy, along with a percentage of the daughters, so that although the line will ramify it will not ramify too far. Those are Hendrik's ambitions.

47. Hendrik has found a wife because he is no longer a young man, because he does not wish his blood to die from the earth forever, because he has come to dread nightfall, because man was not made to live alone.

48. I know nothing of Hendrik. The reason for this is that in all our years together on the farm he has kept his station while I have kept my distance; and the combination of the two, the station and the distance, has ensured that my gaze falling on him, his gaze falling on me, have remained kindly, incurious, remote. This passes with me for an explanation. Hendrik is a man who works on the farm. He is nothing but a tall, straight-shouldered brown man with high cheekbones and slanting eyes who crosses the yard with a swift tireless walk I cannot imitate, the legs swivelled from the hip rather than bent at the knee, a man who slaughters the sheep for us on Friday evenings and hangs the carcase in the tree and chops the wood and milks the cow and says, 'Morning, miss,' in the mornings and lifts his hat and goes about his duties. We have our places, Hendrik and I, in an old old code. With fluid ease we move through the paces of our dance.

49. I keep the traditional distance. I am a good mistress, fair-minded, even-handed, kindly, in no sense a witch-woman. To the servants my looks do not count, and I am grateful. Therefore what I feel blowing in on the thin dawn wind is not felt by me alone. All of us feel it, and all of us have grown sombre. I lie awake listening to the cries, muted, stifled, of desire and sorrow and disgust and anguish, even anguish, that swoop and glide and tremble through this house, so that one might think it infested with bats, with anguished, disgusted, sorrowful, longing bats, searching for a lost nesting-place, wailing at a pitch that makes dogs cringe and sears that inner ear of mine which, even in subterranean sleep, tunes itself to my father's signals. It is from his bedroom that the cries have been coming, higher and angrier and sorrier than ever since Hendrik brought back his girl from Armoede, the dust rising lazily behind the cart, the donkeys toiling up the path to the cottage, weary after the long haul. At the door Hendrik pulls up, he rests the whip in its socket and dismounts and lifts the girl down and turning his back on her begins to unharness. And standing here on the

stoep six hundred yards away my father for the first time sees through his heavy field-glasses the red kerchief, the wideset eyes, the pointed chin, the sharp little teeth, the foxy jaw, the thin arms, the slender body of Hendrik's Anna.

50. The great beam of my vision swings and for a spell Hendrik's child-bride is illuminated, stepping down from the donkey-cart. Then, like the lighthouse-keeper strapped into his chair against the treacherous seventh wave; I watch the girl slip back into the dark, hear the grinding of the cogs that turn the lamp, and wait for Hendrik, or my father, or that other woman, to swim into view and glow for a spell with a light that is not their own but comes from me and may even be not light but fire. I have only, I tell myself, to throw off the straps and haul on the lever ready to my hand for the cogs to stop grinding and the light to fall steady on the girl, her slim arms, her slender body; but I am a coward, to speak only of cowardice, the beam swings on, and in a moment I am watching the stone desert or the goats or my face in the mirror, objects on which I can happily release the dry acid breath I have held back so painfully, breath that is, I cannot after all deny it, my spirit, my self, or as much so as the light is. Though I may ache to abdicate the throne of consciousness and enter the mode of being practised by·goats or stones, it is with an ache I do not find intolerable. Seated here I hold the goats and stones, the entire farm and even its environs, as far as I know them, suspended in this cool, alienating medium of mine, exchanging them item by item for my word-counters. A hot gust lifts and drops a flap of ochre dust. The landscape recomposes itself and settles. Then Hendrik hands his bride down from the donkey-cart. Vivid and unwitting under the lenses of the field-glasses she takes her first steps toward the cottage, still holding what may be a withered posy, her toes demurely inward, soft flesh brushing soft flesh under the stiff calico of her skirt, and words again begin to falter. Words are coin. Words alienate. Language is no medium for desire. Desire is rapture, not exchange. It is only by alienating

the desired that language masters it. Hendrik's bride, her sly doe-eyes, her narrow hips, are beyond the grope of words until desire consents to mutate into the curiosity of the watcher. The frenzy of desire in the medium of words yields the mania of the catalogue. I struggle with the proverbs of hell.

51. In the hour before dawn Hendrik wakes, roused by sounds too subtle for my ear, veerings of the wind, the rustlings of birds at the tail-end of sleep. In the dark he puts on his trousers, his shoes, his jacket. He rekindles the fire and brews coffee. Behind his back the stranger pulls up the kaross snug about her ears and lies watching. Her eyes gleam orange. The window is shut, the air in the cottage rich with human smells. They have lain naked all night, waking and sleeping, giving off their complex odours: the smoky sourness of brown people, I know that by heart, I must have had a brown nurse though I cannot recall her; (I sniff again, the other smells are harder) the iron smell of blood certainly; coming piercingly through the blood the thin acrid track of the girl's excitement; and finally, drenching the air with milky sweetness, the flood of Hendrik's response. The question to ask is not, How do I, a lonely spinster, come to know such things? It is not for nothing that I spend evenings humped over the dictionary. Words are words. I have never pretended to embrace that night's experience. A factor, I deal in signs merely. The true question is, If I know these things, then how much the more must my father not know them, and therefore, swelling with envy in its cell, why does the hot shell of his heart not burst? I pick up and sniff and describe and drop, moving from one item to the next, numbering the universe steadily with my words; but what weapons has he with which to keep at bay the dragons of desire? I am no prophetess, but a chill in the wind tells me that disaster is coming. I hear dark footfalls in the empty passages of our house. I hunch my shoulders and wait. After decades of sleep something is going to befall us.

52. Hendrik squats before the fire to pour the boiling water over the coffee-grounds. While the idyll lasts he will make his own coffee. Then the girl, from fairy visitor grown to wife, will learn to get up first, and no doubt soon be shouted at and beaten too. Ignorant of this she watches eagerly, rubbing the warm soles of her feet together.

53. Hendrik steps out into the last of the night-world. In the trees along the riverbed birds begin to grow restless. The stars are clear as ice. The pebbles grate crisply under his shoes. I hear the clank of the pail against the stone floor of the store-room, then his swift stride crunching away to the cowshed. My father tosses his blankets aside, swings out of bed, and stands on the cold floor in his socks. In my own room I am already dressing, for I must have his coffee ready when, stern and drawn, he stamps into the kitchen. Life on the farm.

54. No word about the marriage has passed between Hendrik and my father since the day when Hendrik came to ask leave to bring a wife on to the farm and my father replied, 'Do as you wish.' The wedding-feast was held at Armoede, the wedding-night on the road or here, I do not know, and the day after that Hendrik was back at work. My father increased his rations but offered no wedding-gift. The first time I saw Hendrik after the announcement I said, 'Congratulations, Hendrik,' and he touched his hat and smiled and said, 'Thank you, miss.'

55. Sitting on the stoep side by side, watching the last of the sunset, waiting for shooting-stars, we sometimes hear the twang of Hendrik's guitar-strings, fumbling, gentle, across the river. One night when the air was particularly still we heard him pick his way through the whole of *Hand vol vere*. But most nights the wind whips the frail sounds away, and we might as well be on separate planets, we on ours, they on theirs.

56. I see little of Hendrik's bride. While he is away she keeps to the cottage, foraying only to the dam for water or to the river for firewood, where my eye is unfailingly drawn to her scarlet kerchief bobbing among the trees. She is familiarizing herself with her new life, with the routine of cooking and washing, with her duties to her husband, with her own body, with the four walls around her, with the view from the front door and the great whitewashed farmhouse that lies at the centre of that view, with the heavy man and the brisk, thin woman who come out on the stoep in the evenings and sit staring into space.

57. Hendrik and his wife visit Jakob and Anna on Sundays. They put on their best clothes, span in the donkeys, and trundle sedately down the half-mile of track to the old schoolhouse. I ask Anna about the girl. She says she is 'sweet' but still a child. If she is a child, what am I? I see that Anna would like to take her under her wing.

58. Hat in hand, Hendrik stands at the kitchen door waiting for me to look up. Across the batter-bowl and the broken eggshells I meet his eyes.

'Good morning, miss.'

'Good morning, Hendrik. How are you?'

'We are well, miss. I came to ask: does miss perhaps have work in the house? For my wife, miss.'

'Yes, perhaps I have, Hendrik. But where is your wife?'

'She is here, miss.' He nods back over his shoulder, then finds my eyes again.

'Tell her to come inside.'

He turns and says '*Hê*!' smiling tightly. There is a flash of scarlet and the girl slips behind him. He steps aside, leaving her framed in the doorway, hands clasped, eyes downcast.

'So you are another Anna. Now we have two Annas.'

She nods, still averting her face.

'Talk to the miss!' whispers Hendrik. His voice is harsh, but

31

that means nothing, we all know, such are the games we play for each other.

'Anna, miss,' whispers Anna. She clears her throat softly.

'Then you will have to be Klein-Anna – we can't have two Annas in the same kitchen, can we?'

She is beautiful. The head and eyes are childishly large, the lines of lip and cheekbone clear as if outlined in pencil. This year, and next year, and perhaps the next, you will still be beautiful, I say to myself, until the second child comes, and the childbearing and the ailments and the squalor and monotony exhaust you, and Hendrik feels betrayed and bitter, and you and he begin to shout at each other, and your skin creases and your eyes dull. You will be like me yet, I tell myself, never fear.

'Look at me, Anna, don't be shy. Would you like to come and work in the house?'

She nods slowly, rubbing her instep with her big toe. I watch her toes and her wiry calves.

'Come on, child, speak, I won't eat you up!'

'Hê!' whispers Hendrik from the door.

'Yes, miss,' she says.

I advance on her, drying my hands on my apron. She does not flinch, but her eyes flicker toward Hendrik. I touch her under the chin with my forefinger and lift her face.

'Come, Anna, there is nothing to be afraid of. Do you know who I am?'

She looks straight into my eyes. Her mouth is trembling. Her eyes are not black but dark dark brown, darker even than Hendrik's.

'Well, who am I?'

'Miss is the miss.'

'Well, come on then! . . . Anna!'

But Anna, my old Anna, has, it seems, been hovering in the passage all the time, listening.

'Anna, this is our Klein-Anna. You are so nice and big: what if we make you Ou-Anna, then she can be Klein-Anna. How does that sound?'

'That sounds fine, miss.'

'Now listen: give her a mug of tea, then she can get down to work. Show her where the things for scrubbing are kept, I want her to scrub the kitchen floor first of all. And you, Klein-Anna, you must see to it that you bring your own mug and plate tomorrow. Will you remember?'

'Yes, miss.'

'Hendrik, you must go now, the baas will be cross if he sees you hanging around here.'

'Yes, miss. Thank you, miss.'

All of this in our own language, a language of nuances, of supple word-order and delicate particles, opaque to the outsider, dense to its children with moments of solidarity, moments of distance.

59. It rained this morning. For days there had been rainclouds rolling in trains across the sky from horizon to horizon, and far-off thunder rattling against the dome of space, and a sultry gloom. Then at mid-morning the birds began to circle and settle and give muted nesting calls. All breath of air ceased. Drops of water, huge, lukewarm, splashed straight down out of the sky, faltered, then began to fall in earnest as the thunderstorm, laced with lightning and endlessly resonating, cut a path across us moving northward. For an hour it rained. Then it was over, birds sang, the earth steamed, the last fresh runnels dwindled and sank away.

60. Today I darned six pairs of socks for my father. There is a convention older than myself which says that Anna should not do the darning.

61. Today's leg of mutton was excellent: tender, juicy, roasted to a turn. There is a place for all things. Life is possible in the desert.

62. Coming over the rise past the dam, my father gathers about

33

his head and shoulders the streaks and whorls, orange, pink, lavender, mauve, crimson, of the haloed sunset display. Whatever it is that he has been doing today (he never says, I never ask), he comes home nevertheless in pride and glory, a fine figure of a man.

63. In the face of all the allures of sloth, my father has never ceased to be a gentleman. When he goes out riding he wears his riding-boots, which I must help him off with and which Anna must wax. On his inspection tour every second week he wears a coat and tie. In a stud-box he keeps three collar-studs. Before meals he washes his hands with soap. He drinks his brandy ceremonially, by himself, from a brandy-glass, of which he has four, by lamplight, sitting in an armchair. Every month, stiff as a ramrod on a stool outside the kitchen door, the chickens eyeing him and clucking, he subjects himself to the discipline of my cutting-scissors. I trim the iron-grey hair, smoothing it with the palm of my hand. Then he stands up, shakes out the napkins, thanks me, and stalks away. Who would think that out of rituals like these he could string together day after day, week after week, month after month, and, it would seem, year after year, riding in every evening against a flaming sky as though he had spent the whole day waiting for this moment, his horse tethered in a thorn-tree's shade just over the rise, he reclining against the saddle, whittling clothespegs, smoking, whistling through his teeth, dozing with his hat over his eyes, his pocket-watch in his hand. Is that the extent of the hidden life he leads when he is out of sight, or is the thought irreverent?

64. Every sixth day, when our cycles coincide, his cycle of two days, my cycle of three, we are driven to the intimacy of relieving our bowels in the bucket-latrine behind the fig-trees in the malodour of the other's fresh faeces, either he in my stench or I in his. Sliding aside the wooden lid I straddle his hellish gust, bloody, feral, the kind that flies love best, flecked,

I am sure, with undigested flesh barely mulled over before pushed through. Whereas my own (and here I think of him with his trousers about his knees, screwing his nose as high as he can while the blowflies buzz furiously in the black space below him) is dark, olive with bile, hard-packed, kept in too long, old, tired: We heave and strain, wipe ourselves in our different ways with squares of store-bought toilet paper, mark of gentility, recompose our clothing, and return to the great outdoors. Then it becomes Hendrik's charge to inspect the bucket and, if it prove not to be empty, to empty it in a hole dug far away from the house, and wash it out, and return it to its place. Where exactly the bucket is emptied I do not know; but somewhere on the farm there is a pit where, looped in each other's coils, the father's red snake and the daughter's black embrace and sleep and dissolve.

65. But the patterns change. My father has begun to come home in the mornings. Never before has he done this. He blunders into the kitchen and makes tea for himself. Me he shrugs away. He stands with his hands in his pockets, his back to the two Annas, if they are there, looking out of the window, while the tealeaves draw. The maids hunch their shoulders, disquieted, obliterating themselves. Of if they are not there he wanders through the house cup in hand until he finds Klein-Anna, sweeping or polishing or whatever, and stands over her, watching, saying nothing. I hold my tongue. When he leaves we women all relax.

66. In this bare land it is hard to keep secrets. We live naked beneath each other's hawk-eyes, but live so under protest. Our resentment of each other, though buried in our breasts, sometimes rises to choke us, and we take long walks digging our fingernails into our palms. It is only by whelming our secrets in ourselves that we can keep them. If we are tight-lipped it is because there is much in us that wants to burst out. We search for objects for our anger and, when we find them, rage immod-

erately. The servants dread my father's rages, always in excess of their occasion. Goaded by him, they lash the donkeys, throw stones at the sheep. How fortunate that beasts feel no anger, but endure and endure! The psychology of masters.

67. While Hendrik is out on a godforsaken task in the heat of the afternoon my father visits his wife. He rides up to the door of the cottage and waits, not dismounting, till the girl comes out and stands before him squinting against the sun. He speaks to her. She is bashful. She hides her face. He tries to soothe her. Perhaps he even smiles, but I cannot see. He leans down and gives her a brown paper packet, It is full of candies, hearts and diamonds with mottoes on them. She stands holding the packet while he rides away.

68. Or: As Klein-Anna makes her way homeward in the heat of the afternoon my father comes upon her. She stops while, bending over the horse's neck, he speaks to her. She is bashful and hides her face. He tries to soothe her, even smiling at her. From his pocket he takes a brown paper packet, which he gives her. It is full of candies, what they call hearts and diamonds. She folds the packet small and walks on.

69. He bends over the horse's neck, talking to the girl, trying to soothe her. She hides her face. He reaches into his pocket and I catch a flash of silver. For an instant the coin lies open in her palm, a shilling or even a florin. They both look at it. Then the hand closes. He rides off and she walks home.

70. He pecks at his food and pushes it away. He drinks his glass of brandy not sitting in his armchair but pacing about the yard in the moonlight. His voice, when he speaks to me, is gruff with defiance and shame. I do not need to lurk behind the shutters to know his guilty thoughts.

71. Where can she possibly spend the money? Where will she

hide it from her husband? Where will she hide the sweets? Or will she eat them all herself in a single day? Is she so much of a child? If she has one secret from her husband she will soon have two. Cunning, cunning gift!

72. He believes that he will begin to prosper once I am out of the way. Though he dare not say so, he would like me to take to my bedchamber with a migraine and stay there. I am prepared to believe he is sincere when he says to himself that he wishes I and Hendrik and all the other hindrances would go away. But how long does he think their idyll will last, the two of them alone on the farm, an ageing man and a servant-girl, a silly child? He will be maddened by the vacuous freedom of it. What will they do together day after day after day? What can they have to say to each other? The truth is that he needs our opposition, our several oppositions, to hold the girl away from him, to confirm his desire for her, as much as he needs our opposition to be powerless against that desire. It is not privacy that he truly wants, but the helpless complicity of watchers. Nor can I believe that he does not know how he enters my dreams, in what capacities, committing what acts. The long passage that links the two wings of the house, with his bedroom in one wing and mine in the other, teems with nocturnal spectres, he and I among them. They are not my creatures nor are they his: they are ours together. Through them we possess and are possessed by each other. There is a level, we both know, at which Klein-Anna is a pawn and the real game lies between the two of us.

73. I have given in to his wish and announced my indisposition. The green shutters are locked. All day I lie stretched out on the counterpane with my horny toes in the air and a pillow over my eyes. Everything I need is here: under the bed a pot, by the bedside a carafe of water with a tumbler over the neck. Old Anna brings the meals and cleans the room. I eat like a bird. I take nothing for the migraine, knowing that nothing

will help me and being anyhow a cultist of pain. Pleasure is hard to come by, but pain is everywhere these days, I must learn to subsist on it. The air is cool and green even in the afternoons. Sometimes the pain is a solid block behind the wall of my forehead, sometimes a disk within my skull tilting and humming with the movements of the earth, sometimes a wave that unrolls and thuds endlessly against the backs of my eyelids. I lie hour after hour concentrating on the sounds inside my head. In a trance of absorption I hear the pulse in my temples, the explosion and eclipse of cells, the grate of bone, the sifting of skin into dust. I listen to the molecular world inside me with the same attention I bring to the prehistoric world outside. I walk in the riverbed and hear the cascade of thousands of grains of sand, or smell the iron exhalation of rocks in the sun. I bring my understanding to the concerns of insects – the particles of food that must be carried over mountaintops and stored in holes, the eggs that must be arranged in hexagons, the rival tribes that must be annihilated. The habits of birds, too, are stable. It is therefore with reluctance that I confront the gropings of human desire. Clenched beneath a pillow in a dim room, focussed on the kernel of pain, I am lost in the being of my being. This is what I was meant to be: a poetess of interiority, an explorer of the inwardness of stones, the emotions of ants, the consciousness of the thinking parts of the brain. It seems to be the only career, if we except death, for which life in the desert has fitted me.

74. My father is exchanging forbidden words with Klein–Anna. I do not need to leave my room to know. *We*, he is saying to her, *we two*: and the word reverberates in the air between them. *Now: come with me now*, he is saying to her. There are few enough words true, rock-hard enough to build a life on, and these he is destroying. He believes that he and she can choose their words and make a private language, with an *I* and *you* and *here* and *now* of their own. But there can be no private language. Their intimate *you* is my *you* too. Whatever they may say to

each other, even in the closest dead of night, they say in common words, unless they gibber like apes. How can I speak to Hendrik as before when they corrupt my speech? How do I speak to them?

75. Days and nights wheel past, the light in my shuttered room brightens to grey-green and darkens to black, old Anna appears and disappears and reappears in a round of pot and plate, murmuring, clucking. I lie here involved in cycles of time, outside the true time of the world, while my father and Hendrik's wife travel their arrow-straight paths from lust to capture, from helplessness to the relief of surrender. Now they are past cajolements and gifts and shy shakings of the head. Hendrik is ordered to the remotest marches of the farm to burn the ticks off sheep. My father tethers his horse outside his servant's house. He locks the door behind him. The girl tries to push his hands off, but she is awed by what is about to happen. He undresses her and lays her out on his servant's coir mattress. She is limp in his arms. He lies with her and rocks with her in an act which I know enough about to know that it too breaks codes.

76. 'I look upon any poor man as totally undone,' whispers a voice (in my solitude I hear voices, perhaps I am truly a witch-woman), ' . . . totally undone if he has the misfortune to have an honest heart, a fine wife, and a powerful neighbour.' Poor Hendrik: undone, undone. I weep drunken weeping. Then I screw my eyes tight against the pain and wait for the three figures to dissolve into streaks and pulses and whorls: Hendrik playing his mouthorgan beneath a far-off thorn-tree, the couple clenched in the stifling hut. There is finally only I, drifting into sleep, beyond the reach of pain. Acting on myself I change the world. Where does this power end? Perhaps that is what I am trying to find out.

77. Anna has not come. All morning I have lain waiting for

her discreet tap at the door. I think of tea and rusks and my saliva flows. There is no doubt about it, I am not pure spirit.

78. I stand in my slippers in the empty kitchen, dizzy after my long hibernation. The stove is cold. The sun blinks on the rows of copperware.

79. I stand behind my chair, gripping the back, and speak to my father.

'Where is Anna? She has not been in today.'

He forks up a mouthful of rice and gravy, bending over his plate. He chews with appetite.

'Anna? How should I know where Anna is? It's none of my business. The maids are your business. Which Anna are you talking about?'

'I'm talking about our Anna. Our Anna, not the other one. I want to know where she is. The schoolhouse is empty.'

'They have gone. They left this morning.'

'Who has gone?'

'She and old Jakob. They took the donkey-cart.'

'And why have they suddenly left? Why didn't you tell me? Where have they gone?'

'They have gone. They asked me, and I said they could. What else do you want to know?'

'Nothing. There is nothing more I want to know.'

80. Or perhaps as I come into the room words are already issuing from that towering black cylinder.

'Anna and Jakob have gone. I have given them a holiday. You will have to get along without Anna for a while.'

81. Or perhaps there is only the empty kitchen, and the cold stove, and the rows of gleaming copperware, and absence, two absences, three absences, four absences. My father creates absence. Wherever he goes he leaves absence behind him. The absence of himself above all – a presence so cold, so dark,

so remote as to be itself an absence, a moving shadow casting a blight on the heart. And the absence of my mother. My father is the absence of my mother, her negative, her death. She the soft, the fair; he the hard, the dark. He has murdered all the motherly in me and left me this brittle, hairy shell with the peas of dead words rattling in it. I stand in the empty kitchen hating him.

82. The past. I grope around inside my head for the mouth of the tunnel that will lead me back in time and memory past images of myself younger and younger, fresher and fresher, through youth and childhood back to my mother's knee and my origins, but the tunnel is not there. Inside my skull the walls are glassy, I see only reflections of myself drab and surly staring back at myself. How can I believe this creature was ever a child, how can I believe she was born of humankind? Easier to imagine her crawling from under a stone in her bottlegreen sheath, licking the egg-slime off herself before taking her bearings and crawling off to this farmhouse to take up residence behind the wainscot.

83. But perhaps if I spend a day in the loft emptying old trunks I will find evidence of a credible past: ornamental fans, lockets and cameos, dancing slippers, favours and souvenirs, a baptismal frock, and photographs, if there were photographs in those days, daguerrotypes perhaps, showing a scowling baby with its hair in curls sitting in the lap of a woman, hesitant, obscure, and behind them the stiff figure of a man, and, who knows, beside them a scowling lad too, in a suit trimmed with lace, a brother who must have died in one of the great epidemics, the influenza epidemic or the smallpox epidemic, leaving me without a protector. And then, in the bloom of her tentative young motherhood, the woman must have died trying to give birth to a third child, died as she feared she would, afraid to deny the man his detested relentless pleasure in her, her death

a hideous storm of terror, with the midwife wringing her hands about the room and recommending ipecacuanha as a last resort.

84. All over this land there must be patient middle-aged children waiting for their parents' grip on the keys to slacken. The day I compose my father's hands on his breast and pull the sheet over his face, the day I take over the keys, I will unlock the rolltop desk and uncover all the secrets he has kept from me, the ledgers and banknotes and deeds and wills, the photographs of the dead woman inscribed 'With all my love', the packet of letters tied in a red ribbon. And in the darkest corner of the bottommost pigeonhole I will uncover the onetime ecstasies of the corpse, the verses folded three and four times and packed into a manila envelope, the sonnets to Hope and Joy, the confessions of love, the passionate vows and dedications, the postmarital rhapsodies, the quatrains 'To my Son': and then no more, silence, the vein petering out. At some point on the line from youth to man to husband to father to master the heart must have turned to stone. Was it there, with the advent of the stunted girl? Was I the one who killed the life in him, as he kills the life in me?

85. In grotesque pink slippers I stand in the centre of the kitchen floor. My eyes pinch against the stab of the sunlight. Behind me lies the haven of the bed in the darkened room, before me the irritation of a day's housework. How can I possibly, out of the somnolence and banality of my life, out of ignorance and incapacity, whip up the menace of an outraged daughter confronting an abashed or arrogant father, a brazen or trembling servant-girl? My heart is not in it, nothing has prepared me for this part. Life in the desert teaches nothing if not that all things are permissible. I want no more than to creep back into bed and fall asleep with my thumb in my mouth, or else to search out my oldest sunbonnet and wander away down the riverbed till the house is out of sight and I hear nothing but the cicadas thrilling and the flies whipping past my face.

My theme is the endless drift of the currents of sleep and waking, not the storms of human conflict. Where this house stands in the desert there is a turbulence, a vortex, a black hole that I live in but abhor. I would have been far happier under a bush, born in a parcel of eggs, bursting my shell in unison with a thousand sisters and invading the world in an army of chopping mandibles. Between four walls my rage is baffled. Reflected from planes of plaster and tile and board and wallpaper, my outpourings rain back on me, stick to me, seep back through my skin. Though I may look like a machine with opposed thumbs that does housework, I am in truth a sphere quivering with violent energies, ready to burst upon whatever fractures me. And while there is one impulse in me that tells me to roll out and erupt harmlessly in the great outdoors, I fear that there is another impulse – I am full of contradictions – telling me to hide in a corner like a black widow spider and engulf whoever passes in my venom. 'Take that for the youth I never had!' I hiss, and spit, if spiders can spit.

86. But the truth is that I have worn black widow-weeds longer than I can remember, for all I know I was a baby in a black diaper waving my rickety little legs, clutching at my black knitted bootees, wailing. Certainly at the age of six I was wearing, day in, day out, a hideous bottlegreen frock that draped me from throat to wrists and revealed the merest flash of meagre shins before these were engulfed in black clubshoes. I must have been photographed at that age, I have no other explanation for it; there must be a photograph of me in one of those trunks or desks, and I must have missed it when I was listing the items. How could a mere child have had enough self-awareness to see herself with such dispassionate clarity, down to the pinched mouth and the pallor and the rat's-tail of hair? Or perhaps I had a vision, I must not rely too much on photographs, what could all those photographers have been doing in the desert when I was a child, not hunting me I am sure; perhaps, being a brooding kind of child, I was transported out

of myself for an instant and had a vision of myself as I really was, in my bottlegreen dress, which must surely also be in the loft, stuck away somewhere, before I was returned to my unthinking animal integrity by whoever it was that vouchsafed me the vision, my tutelary angel, or some other variety of angel, a variety that warns one against high hopes for oneself perhaps, an angel of reality, a salutary angel. Or perhaps I never had animal integrity, or lost it before I was six, perhaps by the age of six I was already a little corporal machine trotting around the yard, building enclosures of stones or whatever it is that children do, pulling the wings off flies, watched over gravely by a little ghostly double; perhaps, regrettably, there are no angels, perhaps all the snapshots of my childish self that I carry about with me are the work of that little watcher (what else had she to do?), perhaps she split off from me when I was very very young, perhaps even my vision of myself as a baby with heartburn or heartache or whatever, clutching at my black bootees and wailing, is a vision of that double, pondering by the cribside, feeling her own ghostly heartache, I guess of course that it was a she, besides seeing blind alleys bifurcating everywhere, which I ignore, being after bigger things than problems of philosophy.

87. I am a black widow in mourning for the uses I was never put to. All my life I have been left lying about, forgotten, dusty, like an old shoe, or when I have been used, used as a tool, to bring the house to order, to regiment the servants. But I have quite another sense of myself, glimmering tentatively some-where in my inner darkness: myself as a sheath, as a matrix, as protectrix of a vacant inner space. I move through the world not as a knifeblade cutting the wind, or as a tower with eyes, like my father, but as a hole, a hole with a body draped around it, the two spindly legs hanging loose at the bottom and the two bony arms flapping at the sides and the big head lolling on top. I am a hole crying to be whole. I know this is in one sense just a way of speaking, a way of thinking about myself, but if

one cannot think of oneself in words, in pictures, then what is there to think of oneself in? I think of myself as a straw woman, a scarecrow, not too tightly stuffed, with a scowl painted on my face to scare the crows and in my centre a hollow, a space which the fieldmice could use if they were very clever. But this is more than a picture, I cannot deny it, I am not ignorant of anatomy, I am not incurious about my constitution, I am among other things a farmgirl living in the midst of the hurlyburly of nature, or such paltry hurlyburly as we have in the desert, not unaware that there is a hole between my legs that has never been filled, leading to another hole never filled either. If I am an O, I am sometimes persuaded, it must be because I am a woman. Yet how galling, after meditations that would do credit to a thinker, to find myself worked into the trap of conceding that if only I had a good man to sleep at my side, and give me babies, all would be well, I would perk up and learn to smile, my limbs would fill out, my skin glow, and the voice inside my head stutter and stumble into silence. I do not have it in me to believe that the mating of farmboy with farmgirl will save me, whatever save may mean, at least for the time being, there is no knowing what shifts I may be driven to. Provisionally, I believe myself reserved for a higher fate. Therefore if by a miracle one of the rawboned neighbours should come trotting along one day with a posy of veld-flowers, blushing and sweating, to court me for my inheritance, I will take to my bed or read to him from my terrible sonnets or writhe at his feet in a fit, anything to send him galloping off; always assuming that we have neighbours, I see no evidence of it, we might as well be living on the moon.

88. On the other hand, I have been able, sometimes for days on end, to lose my sense of election, to see myself as simply a lonely, ugly old maid, capable of redemption, to some extent, from loneliness, from loneness, by marriage, a human institution, to another lone soul, a soul perhaps greedier than most, stupider, uglier, not much of a catch, but then what kind of

catch am I; whom I would vow to bend to a little lower, slave for a little harder than another woman would, whom I would have to disrobe for on Saturday nights, in the dark, so as not to alarm him, and arouse, if the arts of arousal can be learned, and guide to the right hole, rendered penetrable with a gob of chickenfat from a pot at the bedside, and endure the huffing and puffing of, and be filled eventually, one expects, with seed by, and lie listening to the snoring of, till the balm of slumber arrive. What I lack in experience I plainly make up for in vision; if the commerce of men with women is not like that it might as well be. I can imagine too falling pregnant after many moons, though it would not astonish me if I were barren, I look like the popular notion of the barren woman, and then, after seven or eight months, giving birth to a child, with no midwife and my husband blind drunk in the next room, gnawing through the umbilical cord, clapping the livid babyface to my flat sour breast; and then, after a decade of closeted breeding, emerging into the light of day at the head of a litter of ratlike, runty girls, all the spit image of myself, scowling into the sun, tripping over their own feet, identically dressed in bottlegreen smocks and snubnosed black shoes; and then, after another decade of listening to their hissing and clawing, packing them off one by one to the outside world to do whatever it is that unprepossessing girls do there, live in boarding-houses and work in post offices perhaps, and bear illegitimate ratchildren to send back to the farm for sanctuary.

89. Perhaps that is all that election means to me: not to have to figure in a bucolic comedy like the above, not to be explained away by poverty, degeneracy, torpor, or sloth. I want my story to have a beginning, a middle, and an end, not the yawning middle without end which threatens no less if I connive at my father's philandering and live to guard his dotage than if I am led to the altar by a swain and die full of years, a wizened granny in a rocking-chair. I must not fall asleep in the middle of my life. Out of the blankness that surrounds me I must pluck

the incident after incident after incident whose little explosions keep me going. For the other kind of story, the weave of reminiscence in the dozing space of the mind, can never be mine. My life is not past, my art cannot be the art of memory. What will happen to me has not yet happened. I am a blind spot hurtling with both eyes open into the maw of the future, my password 'And then?' And if at this instant I do not look as if I am hurtling, it is only because I dither for a while in the empty house, feeling the comfort of the sunlight glancing off the same rows of copperware it glanced off before I was born into this world. I would not be myself if I did not feel the seductions of the cool stone house, the comfortable old ways, the antique feudal language. Perhaps, despite my black clothes and the steel in my heart (unless it is stone, who can tell when it is so far away), I am a conserver rather than a destroyer, perhaps my rage at my father is simply rage at the violations of the old language, the correct language, that take place when he exchanges kisses and the pronouns of intimacy with a girl who yesterday scrubbed the floors and today ought to be cleaning the windows.

90. But this, like so much else about me, is only theory. Let me at all costs not immure myself in a version of myself as avenger, eyes flashing and sword on high, of the old ways. It is the hermit crab, I remember from a book, that as it grows migrates from one empty shell to another. The grim moralist with the fiery sword is only a stopping-place, a little less temporary than the haggard wife knitting on the stoep, a little more temporary than the wild woman of the veld who talks to her friends the insects and walks in the midday sun, but temporary all the same. Whose shell I presently skulk in does not matter, it is the shell of a dead creature. What matters is that my anxious softbodied self should have a refuge from the predators of the deep, from the squid, the shark, the baleen whale, and whatever else it is that preys on the hermit crab, I do not know the oceans, though one day when I am a widow or a monied

47

spinster I promise myself I will spend a day at the seaside, I will pack a basket with sandwiches and fill my purse with money and climb aboard the train and tell the man I want to see the sea: that gives you some idea of how naive I am. I will take off my shoes and crunch through the seasand, wondering at the millions of tiny deaths that have gone to make it up, I will roll up my skirts and wade in the shallows and be nipped by a crab, a hermit crab, as a cosmic joke, and stare at the horizon, and sigh at the immensity of it all, and eat my sandwiches, barely tasting the crisp sourdough bread, the sweet green fig preserve, and think on my insignificance. Then, chastened, sober, I will catch the train back home and sit on the stoep and watch the flaming sunsets, the crimsons, the pinks, the violets, the oranges, the bloody reds, and heave a sigh and sink my head on my breast and weep hesperian tears for myself, for the life I have not lived, the joy and willingness of an unused body now dusty, dry, unsavoury, for the slowing pulse of my blood. I will get up out of the canvas chair and trail off to my bedroom and undress by the last light, saving paraffin, and sighing, sighing fall at once asleep. I will dream of a stone, a pebble lying on the beach, on the acres of white sand, looking into the benign blue sky, lulled by the waves; but whether I will really have had the dream I will never know, for all nightly happenings will be washed from my memory with the crowing of the cock. Or perhaps I shall not sleep at all, but lie tossing and turning with the toothache after all those sugary figs; for we pay no heed to hygiene here, but walk around with foul-smelling breath and in due course with rotten stumps of teeth, wondering what to do with ourselves, until at last we are driven to the extremity of the farrier's tongs, or to oil of cloves on a matchstick, or to weeping. Weeping I have avoided hitherto, but there is a time and a place for everything; I am sure it will come to weeping one day when I am left alone on the farm, when they have all gone, Hendrik and his wife, Anna and Jakob, my father, my mother, the ratlike grandchildren, and I can wander about the house carefree in my shift, and out into the yard, and into the deserted sheep-runs, and into the hills: then will be a time for weeping and for tearing my hair and gnashing my gums without fear of detection or reprisal, without having to keep up a front. That will be the time for testing these lungs I have never tested, to hear whether they can make the hills echo, and the flats, if flats can echo, with their shrieks and groans and laments. That too, who knows, may be the time for tearing up my clothes, for building a great bonfire in front of the house of clothes and furniture and pictures, my father and my mother and my long-lost brother crinkling in the flames among the antimacassars, and for screaming with wild glee as the flames soar into the night sky, and even perhaps for carrying firebrands into the house, for firing the mattresses and the wardrobes and the yellowwood ceilings and the loft with its trunks full of mementos, until even the neighbours, whoever they may be, see the tower of flames on the horizon and come galloping through the darkness to bear me off to a place of safety, a cackling, gibbering old woman who wanted notice taken of her.

91. The schoolhouse is empty. The ashes in the grate are cold. The rack above the stove is bare. The bed is stripped. The shutter flaps. Jakob and Anna are gone. They have been sent packing. They have gone without even speaking to me. I watch the motes of dust dreamily ascend a shaft of sunlight. There is what tastes like blood at the back of my nose but is not. Truly, events have a power to move unmatched by one's darkest imaginings. I stand in the doorway breathing fast.

92. The schoolhouse. Once upon a time this was a real school-house. Children came from the homestead to sit here and learn the three Rs. In summer they yawned and stretched and fidgeted while the heat buzzed in their ears. On winter mornings they picked their way across the frosty earth and chafed chilled bare toes together during the psalm-singing. The children of the neighbours came too, paying in cash and kind. There was

a schoolmistress, daughter of an impoverished clergyman, no doubt, sent out to earn a living. Then one day she ran away with a passing Englishman and was never heard of again. After that there were no more schoolmistresses. For many years the schoolhouse stood unused, bats and starlings and spiders gradually taking it over, until one day it was turned over to Anna and Jakob, or to the Anna and Jakob who came before them, to live in. It cannot be otherwise, if I am simply sucking this history out of my thumb how am I to explain those three wooden benches stacked at the far end of the room, and the easel behind them on which Jakob used to hang his coat? Someone must have built and stocked a schoolhouse, and advertised for a schoolmistress in the *Weekly Advertiser* or the *Colonial Gazette*, and met her train, and installed her in the guestroom, and paid her stipend, in order that the children of the desert should not grow up barbarian but be heirs of all the ages familiar with the rotation of the earth, Napoleon, Pompeii, the reindeer herds of the frozen wastes, the anomalous expansion of water, the seven days of Creation, the immortal comedies of Shakespeare, geometric and arithmetic progressions, the major and minor modes, the boy with his finger in the dyke, Rumpelstiltskin, the miracle of the loaves and the fishes, the laws of perspective, and much much more. But where has it all gone now, this cheerful submission to the wisdom of the past? How many generations can have intervened between those children chanting the six times table and my dubious self? Could my father have been one of them? If I hauled those benches into the light would I find, beneath the dust, his initials hacked into the wood with a penknife? But if so, where has all the humane learning gone? What did he learn from Hansel and Gretel about fathers who lead their daughters into dark forests? What did Noah teach him about fornication? What did the six times table tell him about the iron laws of the universe? And even if it was not he but my grandfather who sat on these benches and sang out his tables, why did he pass on no humanity to my father but leave him a barbarian and me too after him?

Or is it possible that we are not aboriginal here, my line? Did my father or my grandfather perhaps simply gallop up pistolled and bandoliered to the farmhouse one day, out of nowhere, and fling down a tobacco-pouch of gold nuggets, and shoo the schoolmistress out of the schoolhouse, and instal his hinds in her place, and institute a reign of brutishness? Or am I wrong, quite wrong? Was I the one who attended school here, sitting in the darkest corner draped in spiderwebs while my brothers and sisters, my many brothers and sisters, as well as the children from the neighbouring farms, clamoured to have a turn to tell the story of Noah; and have I put them all from my mind utterly, because of their happy laughter, or because they stuffed caterpillars down the back of my bottlegreen smock to punish me for my sour face and my hatred of games; and have they determined nevermore to communicate with me, but to leave me behind with my father in the desert while they make their fortunes in the city? How hard to believe this. If I have brothers and sisters they cannot be in the city, they must all have been swept away by the great meningitis epidemic; for I cannot believe that fraternal intercourse would not have left its mark upon me, and it has all too plainly not left its mark upon me, the mark that has been left upon me instead is the mark of intercourse with the wilds, with solitude and vacancy. Nor can I believe that I was ever told the story of Noah, to speak of Noah only, sitting in a ring with the other children. My learning has the reek of print, not the resonance of the full human voice telling its stories. But perhaps our teacher was not a good teacher, perhaps she slumped sullen at her table tapping the cane in the palm of her hand, brooding over insults, dreaming of escape, while her pupils picked their way through their reading-books and one could hear a pin drop. For how else could I have learned to read, to say nothing of writing?

93. Or perhaps they were stepbrothers, perhaps that explains everything, perhaps that is the truth, it certainly has more of the ring of truth, if I can trust my ear: perhaps they were my

stepbrothers and stepsisters, children of a buxom blonde much-loved wife who passed away in her prime; perhaps, themselves bold and blond and buxom and repelled by all that was shadowy and uncertain, they waged incessant war on the offspring of the mousy unloved second wife who died in childbirth. Then later, having imbibed all that their governess could offer, they were swept off *en masse* by a bluff maternal uncle to live happily ever after, leaving me behind to watch over my father's last years. And I have forgotten this horde not because I hated them but because I loved them and they were taken from me. In my dark corner I used to sit openmouthed devouring their robust gaiety, hoarding up memories of all the shouting and laughter so that in my lonely bed I could relive the day and hug it to me. But of all my stepbrothers and stepsisters it was Arthur I loved most. If Arthur had thrashed me I would have squirmed with pleasure. If Arthur had thrown a stone I would have run to fetch it. For Arthur I would have eaten bootblacking, drunk urine. But alas, golden Arthur never noticed me, occupied as he was with winning the race and catching the ball and reciting the six times table. The day that Arthur left I hid in the darkest corner of the wagonhouse vowing that never another morsel of food would pass my lips. As the years went by and Arthur did not return I thrust his memory farther and farther from me, till today it recurs to me with all the remoteness of a fairy-tale. End of story. There are inconsistencies in it, but I have not the time to track down and abolish them, there is something that tells me I must get out of this schoolhouse and back to my own room.

94. I close the door, sit down, and confront with unweeping eyes the patch of wallpaper above the desk where glows no image of golden Arthur and myself running hand in hand on the seashore, but a pink rose with two green leaves in a field of identical pink roses casting their light eternally into the uncomprehending space of the cubicle and on to the roses on the other walls. This is the irreducible, this is my room (I settle

deep in my chair), and I do not wish that it should ever change: for the comfort of my dark days, the consolation that keeps me from closing my eyes, folding my arms, and rocking myself forever into vacancy, is the knowledge that from me and from me only do these flowers draw the energy that enables them to commune with themselves, with each other, in their ecstasy of pure being, just as the stones and bushes of the veld hum with life, with such happiness that happiness is not the word, because I am here to set them vibrating with their own variety of material awareness that I am forever not they, and they not I, that I can never be the rapture of pure self that they are but am alas forever set off from them by the babble of words within me that fabricate and refabricate me as something else, something else. The farm, the desert, the whole world as far as the horizon is in an ecstasy of communion with itself, exalted by the vain urge of my consciousness to inhabit it. Such are the thoughts I think looking at the wallpaper, waiting for my breath to settle, for the fear to go away. Would that I had never learned to read.

95. But the beast is not enchanted by my prattle. From hour to hour he stalks me through the afternoon. I hear his velvet pad, smell his fetid breath. It is useless, if I go on running I will only perish the more ignominiously, borne down from behind in a cascade of underwear, screaming until my neck is broken, if it is a merciful beast, or until my bowels are clawed out, if it is not. Somewhere on the farm my father roams, burning with shame, ready to strike dead on the spot whoever wags a finger at him. Is my father the beast? Elsewhere on the farm loom Hendrik and Anna, he playing his mouthorgan in the shade of a tree, that is how I still imagine him, she humming to herself, picking her toes, waiting for what is to happen next. Is Hendrik the beast, the insulted husband, the serf trodden under his master's boot, rising to roar for vengeance? Anna, with her sharp little teeth, her hot armpits – is she the beast, the woman, subtle, lascivious, insatiable? I talk and talk to keep

my spirits up while they circle me, smiling, powerful. What is the secret of their power over me? What do they know that I do not know? Whatever way I turn I am blocked. In a month's time, I can see it, I will be bringing my father and my maid breakfast in bed while Hendrik lounges in the kitchen eating biscuits, flicking his claspknife into the tabletop, pinching my bottom as I pass. My father will buy new dresses for her while I wash out her soiled underwear. He and she will lie abed all day sunk in sensual sloth while Hendrik tipples, jackals devour the sheep, and the work of generations falls to ruins. She will bear him olive-skinned children who will pee on the carpets and run up and down the passages. She will conspire with Hendrik to steal his money and his silver watch. They will send for their relatives, brothers and sisters and distant cousins, and settle them on the farm. Through a crack in the shutter I will watch them dance in hordes to guitar music on Saturday nights while the old master sits like an idiot on the stoep smiling and nodding, president of the festival.

96. Who is the beast among us? My stories are stories, they do not frighten me, they only postpone the moment when I must ask: Is it my own snarl I hear in the undergrowth? Am I the one to fear, ravening, immoderate, because here in the heart of the country where space radiates out from me to all the four corners of the earth there is nothing that can stop me? As I sit quietly gazing at my roses waiting for the afternoon to end I find that hard to accept. But I am not quite such a fool as to believe in what I see; and if I attune myself carefully to what is passing inside me I can surely feel far away the withered apple of my womb rise and float, boding all ill. I may be only a ninety-pound spinster crazed with loneliness, but I suspect I am not harmless. So perhaps that is a true explanation of my fear, a fear that is also an expectancy: I fear what I am going to do, nevertheless I am going to do whatever I do because if I do not, but creep away till better days come, my life will continue to be a line trickling from nowhere to nowhere,

without beginning or end. I want a life of my own, just as I am sure my father said to himself he wanted a life of his own when he bought the packet of hearts and diamonds. The world is full of people who want to make their own lives, but to few outside the desert is such freedom granted. Here in the middle of nowhere I can expand to infinity just as I can shrivel to the size of an ant. Many things I lack, but freedom is not one of them.

97. But while I have sat here daydreaming, perhaps even dozing with my cheeks propped on my fists and my gums bared, the afternoon has been sliding away, the light is no longer green but grey, and it is by footsteps and voices that I have been jolted awake. Confused, my heart hammers; foul and sticky from the afternoon's torpor, my mouth floods with salt.

I open the door a crack. The voices are at the far end of the house. One is my father's, issuing commands, I know the tones though I can make out no words. There is a second voice, but I know of it only through the silences of the first.

It is as I feared. The magic of imagining the worst has not worked. The worst is here.

Now those booted feet come up the passage. I close the door and push against it. I have known that tread all my life, yet I stand with mouth agape and pulse drumming. He is turning me into a child again! The boots, the thud of the boots, the black brow, the black eyeholes, the black hole of the mouth from which roars the great NO, iron, cold, thunderous, that blasts me and buries me and locks me up. I am a child again, an infant, a grub, a white shapeless life with no arms, no legs, nothing even to grip the earth with, a sucker, a claw; I squirm, again the boot is raised over me, the mouthhole opens, and the great wind blows, chilling me to my pulpy heart. Though I am leaning against the door he has only to push and I will fall. The core of anger in me is gone, I am afraid, there is no mercy for me, I will be punished and never consoled afterwards. Two minutes ago I was right and he was wrong, I was the dozing fury in the stiff chair waiting to confront him with silence, absence, contempt, and who knows what else; but now I am wrong again, wrong, wrong, wrong as I have been since I was born at the wrong time, in the wrong place, in the wrong body. Tears roll down my cheeks, my nose is stuffed, it is no good, I wait for the man on the other side of the door to decide for me what form tonight's misery is to take.

98. He knocks, three light clicks of fingernail on wood. Salt floods my mouth again; I huddle, holding my breath. Then he goes away: the even footsteps recede one, two, three . . . down the passage. So this is my punishment! He did not want to see me, but to lock me away for the night! Cruel, cruel, cruel! I weep in my cell.

Again the voices come to me. They are in the kitchen. He tells her to put food on the table. She takes bread out of the breadsafe, fat and a bottle of preserves out of the cupboard. He tells her to boil water. She cannot make the paraffin stove work, she tells him. He lights the stove for her. She puts the kettle on the flame. She clasps her hands and waits for the water. He tells her to sit. She is going to sit at table with him. He has cut a slice of bread which he pushes toward her with the point of the knife. He tells her to eat. His voice is gruff. He cannot express tenderness. He expects people to understand this and allow for it. But no one understands it, no one but I, who have sat in corners all my life watching him. I know that his rages and moody silences can only be masks for a tenderness he dare not show lest he be overwhelmed in its consequences. He hates only because he dare not love. He hates in order to hold himself together. He is not a bad man, despite all. He is not unjust. He is merely an ageing man who has had little love and who thinks he has now found it, eating bread and peaches with his girl, waiting for the coffee-water to boil. No scene more peaceful can be imagined, if one ignores the bitter child straining her ears behind the door at the far end of the house. It is a love-feast they are having; but there is one feast which is nobler than the love-feast, and that is the family meal. I should have been invited too. I should be seated at that table, at the foot properly, since I am mistress of the household; and she, not I, should have to fetch and carry. Then we might break bread in peace, and be loving to one another in our different ways, even I. But lines have been drawn, I am excluded from communion, and so this has become a house of two stories, a story of happiness or a lunge toward happiness, and a story of woe.

99. Their spoons tinkle in concert. They have sweet teeth, both of them. Through wisps of steam their eyes meet. Behind her she has a week of knowledge of this strange man, mountainous, hairy, flaccid, decaying, powerful, who tonight comes into the open full of bravado to announce her as his concubine, his property. Does she think of her husband at all, rolled in a blanket beneath the cold stars or groaning in his forlorn cottage, as her new owner's knees enfold her under the table? Does she ask herself how long he will protect her from her husband's anger? Does she think at all about the future, or did she learn at her mother's breast to live and be damned in the luxury of the present? What does this new man mean to her? Does she merely part her thighs, stolid, dull-nerved, because he is the master, or are there refinements of pleasure in subjection which wedded love can never give? Is she giddy with her sudden elevation? Have his gifts intoxicated her, the coins, the candies, whatever he has picked out for her from his wife's aftermath, a feather boa, a rhinestone necklace? Why have those relics never come to me? Why is everything secret from me? Why should I not sit too at the kitchen table smiling and being smiled on in the warm haze of coffee fumes? What is there for me after my purgatory of solitude? Will they wash the dishes before they retire, or will I have to come out in the middle of the night like a cockroach to clean up after them? When will she begin to test her power, when will she sigh and get up from the table and stretch and drift away, leaving the mess for the servant? The day when she does that, will he dare to bark at her, or

will he be so besotted that only the allure of her haunches as she ripples toward their bedroom will have any meaning for him? If she ceases to be the servant who will be the servant but I, unless I run away into the night and never come back, but die in the desert and am picked clean by the birds, followed by the ants, as a reproach? Will he even notice? Hendrik will light on me in his wanderings and bring me back in a sack. They will tip me into a hole and cover me up and say a prayer. Then she will light the fire and put on an apron and wash the dishes, the great mound of dishes, coffee-cup upon coffee-cup, that I left behind, and sigh and begrudge me my death.

—

100. I toss about in the dark whipping myself into distraction. Too much misery, too much solitude makes of one an animal. I am losing all human perspective. Once upon a time I might have shaken off the fit and, pale, tearstained, vacant, dragged myself down the passage to confront them. Then the erotic spell would have been broken, the girl would have slipped out of her chair, my father would have seated me and given me something to drink to restore me. The girl might even have vanished into the night: all would have been well again, the moment postponed when the door clicks shut behind the two of them and I know finally I am excluded from a room I have never been good enough to enter. But tonight I have beaten the waters too long, I am weak, I am tired of telling myself things, tonight I am going to relax, give up, explore the pleasures of drowning, the feel of my body sliding out of me and another body sliding in, limbs inside my limbs, mouth inside my mouth. I welcome death as a version of life in which I will not be myself. There is a fallacy here which I ought to see but will not. For when I wake on the ocean floor it will be the same old voice that drones out of me, drones or bubbles or whatever it is that words do in water. What tedium! When will it ever stop? The moon shines on the black folds of a woman on a cold floor. From her rises like a miasma a fiend of ashen face. The words that whisper through those blue lips

are mine. Drowning, I drown into myself. A phantom, I am no phantom. I stoop. I touch this skin and it is warm, I pinch this flesh and it hurts. What more proof could I want? I am I.

101. I stand outside the door of their room: three bland panels and a china knob over which my hand hovers. They know I am here. The air is alive with my presence. They freeze in their guilty posture, waiting for me to act.

I tap on the door and speak.

'Daddy . . . Can you hear me?'

They are silent, listening to the enormity of their breathing.

'Daddy, I can't sleep.'

They look into each other's eyes, his look saying, What must I do?, her look saying, She is not mine.

'Daddy, I'm feeling strange. What shall I do?'

102. I trail back to the kitchen. Moonlight strikes through the uncurtained window on to the bare table. In the sink lie a plate and two cups waiting to be washed. The coffee-pot is still warm. I could drink coffee too, if I felt like it.

103. I caress the white doorknob. My hand is clammy.

'Daddy . . . Can I say something?'

I turn the knob. The latch moves but the door does not open. They have locked it.

I hear him breathing on the other side of the door. I knock heavily with the side of my fist. He clears his throat and speaks evenly.

'It's late, child. Let us rather talk tomorrow. Go and get some sleep.'

He has spoken. Having found it necessary to lock the door against me, he has now found it necessary to speak to me.

I thump heavily again. What will he do?

The lock snaps open. Through the crack his arm snakes out at me milky white above the dark hair. Instantly he has my wrist in his grasp and crushes it with all the strength of that great hand. I wince, but I will never cry out. What sounds like a cascade of corn-shucks is his whisper, rasping, furious.

'Go to bed! Do you understand what I say?'

'No! I don't feel like sleeping!'

These are not my tears, they are merely tears that pass through me, as the urine I pass is merely urine.

The great hand slides up my arm till it finds and grips my elbow. I am forced down and down; my head is against the doorjamb. I feel no pain. Things are happening in my life, it is better than solitude, I am content.

'Now stop it! Stop irritating me! Go away!'

I am flung back.–The door slams. The key turns.

104. I squat against the wall opposite the door. My head lolls. From my throat comes something which is not a cry, not a groan, not a voice, but a wind that blows from the stars and over the polar wastes and through me. The wind is white, the wind is black, it says nothing.

105. My father stands over me. Clothed, he is his complete masterful self. My dress is rucked up, he can see my knees and the black socks and shoes in which my legs end. I do not, on the whole, care what he sees. The wind still whistles through me, but softly now.

'Come on, child, let's go to bed now.'

The tones are gentle, but I who hear everything hear their angry edge and know how spurious they are.

He catches my wrist and draws my limp puppet-body up. If he lets go I will fall. What happens to this body I do not care. If he wants to stamp it to pulp beneath his heels I will not protest. I am a thing that he holds by the shoulders and steers down the passage to the cell at the farthest end. The passage is endless, our footsteps thunder, the cold wind eats steadily at my face, devouring the tears that drip from me. The wind blows everywhere, it issues from every hole, it turns everything to stone, to the stone, glacial, chilled to the core, of the remotest stars, the stars we shall never see, living their lives from infinity to infinity in darkness and ignorance, if I am not confusing them with planets. The wind blows out of my room, through the keyhole, through the cracks; when that door opens I shall be consumed by it, I shall stand in the mouth of that black vortex without hearing, without touch, engulfed by the wind that roars in the spaces between the atoms of my body, whistles in the cavern behind my eyes.

106. On the familiar green counterpane he lays me down. He lifts my feet and prises my shoes off. He smooths my dress. What more can he do? What more dare he do? Those gentle tones come again.

'Come, sleep now, my child, it is getting late.'

His hand is on my forehead, the horny hand of a man who bends wire. How tender, how comforting! But what he wants to know is whether I am feverish, whether at the root of my desolation lies a microbe. Should I tell him there are no microbes in me, my flesh is too sour to harbour them?

107. He has left me. I lie exhausted while the world spins round and round my bed. I have spoken and been spoken to, touched and been touched. Therefore I am more than just the trace of these words passing through my head on their way from nowhere to nowhere, a streak of light against the void of space, a shooting-star (how full of astronomy I am this evening). So what is the reason that I do not simply turn over and go to sleep as I am, fully dressed, and wake up in the morning and wash the dishes and efface myself and wait for my reward, which must undoubtedly come if justice is to reign in the universe? Alternatively, what is the reason that I do not fall asleep turning over and over in my mind the question of why it is that I do not simply go to sleep as I am, fully dressed?

108. The dinner-bell is in its place on the sideboard. I would have preferred something larger, a loud jangling bell, a school-

bell; perhaps hidden in the loft somewhere is the old school-bell, coated in dust, awaiting the resurrection, if there ever was a school; but I have no time to search it out (though would their hearts not be sent leaping into their mouths if they heard the scuttle of mousepaws, the shuffle of batswings, the ghostly tread of the avenger above their bed?). Quiet as a cat, barefoot, muffling the clapper, I creep up the passage and put my ear to the keyhole. All is silent. Are they lying with bated breath, with two breaths bated, waiting for me to make my move? Are they asleep already? Or are they lying in each other's arms? Is that how it is done, in motions too tiny for the ear to hear, like flies glued together?

109. The bell makes a thin continuous genteel tinkle.

When I am tired of ringing it with the right hand I change it to the left.

I feel better than when I last stood here. I am more tranquil. I begin to hum, at first wavering this side and that of the bell-tone, then finding its level and staying there.

110. Time drifts past, a mist that thins, thickens, and is sucked into the dark ahead. What I think of as my pain, though it is only loneliness, begins to go away. The bones of my face are thawing, I am growing soft again, a soft human animal, a mammal. The bell has found a measure, four soft, four loud, to which I am beginning to vibrate, first the grosser muscles, then the subtler. My woes are leaving me. Small stick-like creatures, they crawl out of me and dwindle.

111. All will yet be well.

112. I am hit. That is what has happened. I am hit a heavy blow on the head. I smell blood, my ears ring. The bell is torn from my hand. I hear it strike the floor, clamorously, far down the passage, and roll left and right as bells do. The passage echoes flatly with shouts which make no sense to me. I slide

down the wall and sit carefully on the floor. Now I can taste the blood. My nose is bleeding. I am swallowing blood; also, when I stick my tongue out, tasting it on my lips.

When was I last struck a blow? I cannot think when. Perhaps I have never been struck before, perhaps I have only been cherished, though that is difficult to believe, cherished and reproved and neglected. The blow does not hurt but it insults. I am insulted and outraged. A moment ago I was a virgin and now I am not, with respect to blows.

The shouting still hangs in the air, like heat, like smoke. If I want to I can reach up and wave my hand in its thickness.

Over me looms a huge white sail. The air is dense with noise. I close my eyes and every other aperture I can. The noise filters into me. I am beginning to jangle. My stomach revolts.

There is another blow, wood on wood. Far, far away a key clatters. The air still rings, though I am by myself.

I have been dealt with. I was a nuisance and now I am dealt with. That is something to think about while I have time on my hands.

I find my old place against the wall, comfortable, hazy, even languorous. Whether, when the thinking begins, it will be thought or dream I cannot guess.

There are vast regions of the world where, if one is to believe what one reads, it is always snowing.

Somewhere, in Siberia or Alaska, there is a field, snow-covered, and in the middle of it a pole, aslant, rotten. Though it may be midday the light is so dim that it could be evening. The snow sifts down endlessly. Otherwise there is nothing as far as the eye can see.

113. In what is properly the hatrack by the front door, in the place where umbrellas would stand if we ever used umbrellas, if our response to rain here were not to lift our faces to it and catch the sultry drops in our mouths and rejoice, stand the two guns, the two-bore shotgun for the partridge and the hare, and

the one known as the Lee-Enfield. The Lee-Enfield is gradu-
ated to 2000 yards. I marvel.

Where the shotgun cartridges are kept I do not know. But
in the little drawer of the hatrack, where they have lain for
years among odd buttons and pins, are six 303 cartridges with
sharp bronze noses. I find them by touch.

One would not think it, looking at me, that I know how to
use a gun, but I do. There are several things about me one
would not think. I am not sure that I can load a magazine in
the dark, but I can slip a single cartridge into the breech and
slide the bolt to. My palms are unpleasantly clammy for
someone who is normally dry to the point of scaliness.

114. I am not easy though I find myself in action. A vacuum
slipped into me somewhere. Nothing that is now happening
satisfies me. I was satisfied while I stood ringing the bell and
humming in the dark, but I doubt that if I went back and groped
about and found the bell under the furniture and wiped off the
cobwebs and stood ringing it and humming I would recover
that happiness. Certain things seem to be forever irrecoverable.
Perhaps that proves the reality of the past.

115. I am not easy. I cannot believe in what is happening to
me. I give my head a shake and suddenly cannot see why I
should not be spending the night in my bed asleep; I cannot
see why my father should not spend the night in his own bed
asleep, and Hendrik's wife the night in her own bed and Hendrik's, asleep. I cannot see a necessity behind what we are doing,
any of us. We are no more than whim, one whim after another.
Why can we not accept that our lives are vacant, as vacant as
the desert we live in, and spend them counting sheep or washing
cups with blithe hearts? I do not see why the story of our lives
should have to be interesting. I am having second thoughts
about everything.

116. The bullet rests snug in its chamber. Wherein does my

own corruption lie? For, having paused for my second thoughts, I will certainly proceed as before. Perhaps what I lack is the resolution to confront not the tedium of pots and pans and the same old pillow every night but a history so tedious in the telling that it might as well be a history of silence. What I lack is the courage to stop talking, to die back into the silence I came from. The history that I make, loading this heavy gun, is only a frantic spurious babble. Am I one of those people so insubstantial that they cannot reach out of themselves save with bullets? That is what I fear as I slip out, an implausible figure, an armed lady, into the starlit night.

117. The yard is awash with silver-blue light. The whitewashed walls of the storehouse and wagonhouse shine with a ghostly pallor. Far away in the lands the blades of the windmill glint. The groan and thud of the piston reaches me faint but clear on the night breeze. The beauty of the world I live in takes my breath away. Similarly, one reads, the scales fall off the eyes of condemned men as they walk to the gallows or the block, and in a moment of great purity, keening with regret that they must die, they yet give thanks for having lived. Perhaps I should change my allegiance from sun to moon.

One sound that I hear, however, does not belong here. Now fainter, now stronger, it is the sound of a distempered dog whining and growling and panting without cease; but it comes not from a dog but from an ape or a human being or several human beings somewhere behind the house.

Holding the gun before me like a tray I tiptoe through the gravel, circling the wagonhouse and coming out in the rear. All along the wall of the house is a bank of shadow. In the shadow against the kitchen door lies whatever it is, not dog or ape but man, in fact (I see as I approach) Hendrik, the one man who ought not to be here. His noise, his babbling, if that is the word, ceases as he sees me. He makes a play of rising as I approach, but falls back. He stretches his hands towards me palms outward.

'Don't shoot!' he says. It is his joke.

My finger does not leave the trigger. I am, for the time being, not to be taken in by appearances. A stench rises from him, not wine but brandy. Only from my father can he have got brandy. Bribed, therefore, not tricked.

With a hand behind him against the kitchen door he tries again to rise. His hat falls out of his lap on to the ground. He stretches for it and collapses slowly on to his side.

'It's me,' he says, putting out his free hand toward the muzzle of the gun, which is far beyond his reach. I take a step back.

Lying on his side on the doorstep with his knees drawn up he forgets me and begins to sob. That, then, is what the noise was. At each tremor his heels give a little kick.

There is nothing I can do for him.

'You are going to get cold, Hendrik,' I say.

118. The door of my father's room is locked against me but the window is open, as ever. I have had enough, tonight, of listening to the sounds that other people make. Therefore it is necessary to act swiftly, without thinking, and, since I cannot plug my ears, to hum softly to myself. I slide the barrel of the rifle between the curtains. Resting the stock on the windowsill I elevate the gun until it points very definitely toward the far ceiling of the room and, closing my eyes, pull the trigger.

I have never been privileged to hear a firearm discharged indoors before. I am used to wave after wave of echoes coming back at me from the hills. But now there is simply the jerk of the butt against my shoulder, the concussion, flat, unremarkable, and then a moment of silence before the first of the screams.

While I listen I sniff in the cordite fumes. Ironstone chipped against ironstone invokes a spark and a wisp of the same heady smoke.

119. In fact I have never heard a scream like this before. It fills the dark chamber with its brilliance and glares through the walls as if they were glass. Exhausting itself in tiny yip-yips, it

bursts open immediately again. I am amazed. I would not have believed one could scream so loudly.

The bolt comes back, the spent case tinkles at my feet, the second cartridge, cool, alien, slips into the breech.

The screams grow shorter, they are acquiring a rhythm. There are also numerous angry lower sounds without rhythm, which I shall separate later, when I have time, if I can recall them.

I elevate the barrel, close my eyes, and pull the trigger. At the same instant the rifle jerks out of my hands. The detonation is even flatter than before. The whole rifle leaves me, surprisingly. It snakes through the curtains and is gone. I rest on my knees empty-handed.

120. I should leave now. I have caused enough trouble, my stomach is unpleasantly excited, the night is spoiled for them, I will undoubtedly have to pay. For the present it would be best if I were by myself.

121. Hendrik stands in the moonlight in the middle of the yard watching me. There is no knowing what he thinks.

In cool, well-formed words I speak to him: 'Go to bed, Hendrik. It is late. Tomorrow is another day.'

He sways, his face shadowed by his hat.

The screaming has devolved into shouting. It would be best for all of us if I left.

I circle Hendrik and take the road that leads away from the farmhouse, or, if one prefers to look at it in another way, that leads into the greater world. At first my back feels vulnerable, but later on less so.

122. Is it possible that there is an explanation for all the things I do, and that that explanation lies inside me, like a key rattling in a can, waiting to be taken out and used to unlock the mystery? Is the following the key: through the agency of conflict with my father I hope to lift myself out of the endless middle

of meditation on unattached existence into a true agon with crisis and resolution? If so, do I wish to employ the key, or do I wish to drop it quietly by the roadside and never see it again? And is it not remarkable how at one moment I can be walking away from a scene of crisis, from gunfire and screaming and interrupted pleasures, my shoes scuffling the pebbles, the moon's rays bearing down on me like bars of silver, the nightbreeze growing chilly, and at the next moment I can be lost to things and back in the gabble of words? Am I, I wonder, a thing among things, a body propelled along a track by sinews and bony levers, or am I a monologue moving through time, approximately five feet above the ground, if the ground does not turn out to be just another word, in which case I am indeed lost? Whatever the case, I am plainly not myself in as clear a way as I might wish. When will I live down tonight's behaviour? I should have kept my peace or been less half-hearted. My distaste for Hendrik's grief showed my half-heart. A woman with red blood in her veins (what colour is mine? a watery pink? an inky violet?) would have pushed a hatchet into his hands and bundled him into the house to search out vengeance. A woman determined to be the author of her own life would not have shrunk from hurling open the curtains and flooding the guilty deed with light, the light of the moon, the light of firebrands. But I, as I feared, hover ever between the exertions of drama and the languors of meditation. Though I pointed the gun and pulled the trigger, I closed my eyes. It was not only a woman's faintness that made me act so, it was a private logic, a psychology which meant to keep me from seeing my father's nakedness. (Perhaps it was this same psychology which made me incapable of reaching out to comfort Hendrik.) (I have said nothing of the girl's nakedness. Why?) There is consolation in having a psychology – for has there ever been a creature blessed with a psychology yet without an existence? – but there is cause for unease too. Whose creature, in a tale of unconscious motives, would I be? My freedom is at risk, I am being worked into a corner by forces beyond my control, there will soon be nothing for me but to sit in a corner weeping and jerking my muscles. It makes no difference that the corner presents itself to me at this moment as a long walk on the open road: at the end of it I shall discover that the earth is round: corners have many shapes. I do not have the equipment for life on the road. That is to say, while I have the feet and legs, and while I would be deceiving myself if I claimed a need for sustenance – with locusts and rain-showers and the odd change of shoes I can go on to infinity – the truth is that I have no stomach for the people I shall meet, the innkeepers and postillions and highwaymen, if that is the century I am in, and the adventures, the rapes and robberies, not that I have anything worth the robbing, not that I have anything worth the raping, that would be a scene to remember, though it happens to the most unexpected people. If, on the other hand, the road is forever as the road is now, dark, winding, stony, if I can stumble along forever in the moonlight or the sunlight, whichever it is to be, without coming out at such places as Armoede or the station or the city where daughters are ruined, if, wonder of wonders, the road goes nowhere day after day, week after week, season after season, except perhaps, if I am lucky, to the lip of the world, then I might give myself to it, to the story of life on the road, without psychology, without adventure, without shape or form, slog slog slog in my old button-shoes, which fall to tatters but are at once replaced by the new button-shoes which hang on a string around my neck like two black breasts, with infrequent stops for locusts and rainwater and even less frequent stops for the calls of nature and yet other stops for slumber and dream-passages, without them we die, and the ribbon of my meditations, black on white, floating like a mist five feet above the ground, stretching back to the horizon, yes, to such a life I might give myself. If I knew that that was all that was required of me my step would quicken at once, my stride lengthen, my hips swing, I would fare forward with a glad heart and a smile. But I have reason to suspect, or perhaps not reason, this sphere is not a sphere of reason, I have a suspicion, a suspicion pure and simple, a groundless suspicion, that this road leads, if I take the right fork, to Armoede location, and if I take the left, to the station. And if I pick my way southward along the cross-ties I will one day find myself at the seaside and be able to walk on the beach listening to the wave-surge, or alternatively to march straight out to sea where, failing a miracle, propelled relentlessly by its ancillary mechanisms, my head will be submerged and the ribbon of words finally trail off forever in a welter of bubbles. And what am I going to say to the folk on the train who look at me so strangely because of the spare shoes around my neck, because of the locusts that spring out of my handbag — the kindly old silver-haired gentleman, the fat lady in black cotton who dabs her perspiring upper lip with the daintiest of handkerchiefs, the stiff youth who looks so intently at me and might at any moment, depending on the century, be revealed as my long-lost brother or my seducer or even both? What words have I for them? I part my lips, they see my mottled teeth, they smell my carious gums, they blanch as there roars at them the old cold black wind that blows from nowhere to nowhere out of me endlessly.

123. My father is sitting on the floor with his back against the footboard of the great double bed in which so much of the engendering in our family has been carried out. To the waist he is naked. His flesh is lilywhite, His face, which ought to be of the same brick-brown as his forearms, is yellow. He is looking straight at me where I stand, hand to mouth, in the first morning light.

The rest of his body is draped in green. He has pulled the green curtains down, the curtain-rod too, that is why the room is so bright. It is the curtain which he is holding around his middle.

We look at each other. Try as I will, I cannot work out what feelings his face expresses. I lack the faculty of reading faces.

124. I go through the house closing doors: two living-room

doors, two dining-room doors, bedroom door, bedroom door, sewing-room door, study door, bathroom door, bedroom door, kitchen door, pantry door, door of my room. Some of the doors are already closed.

125. The cups have not yet been washed.

126. There are flies in my father's room. The air is heavy with their buzzing. They crawl on his face and he does not brush them away, he who has always been a fastidious man. They cluster on his hands, which are red with blood. There are splashes of dried blood on the floor and the curtain is caked with blood. I am not squeamish about blood, I have made blood-sausage on occasion, but in this case I am not sure it would not be better to leave the room for a while, to take a stroll, to clear my head. However, I stay, I am held here.

He speaks, clearing his throat lengthily. 'Fetch Hendrik,' he says. 'Tell Hendrik to come, please.'

He does not resist when I uncurl his fingers from the bloody wad of curtain he holds against himself. In his belly there is a hole big enough to slide my thumb into. The flesh around it is scorched.

His hand catches a corner of the curtain and covers his sex.

It is my fault again I cannot do right. I put the wad back.

127. I am running now as I have not run since childhood, fists clenched, arms pumping, legs toiling through the grey sand of the riverbed. I am wholly involved in my mission, action without reflection, a ninety-pound animal hurling itself through space under the impulse of disaster.

128. Hendrik is asleep on the bare ticking. Bending over him I am overwhelmed with the stench of liquor and urine. Into his dull ear I pant my message: 'Hendrik, wake up, get up! The baas has had an accident! Come and help!'

He flails with his arms, striking me, shouting angry syllables, then falls back into his stupor.

The girl is not here. Where is she?

I begin to hurl things at Hendrik, a kettle, handfuls of spoons and knives, plates. I pick up the broom and ram the bristles into his face. He stumbles from the bed shielding himself with his arms. I thrust and thrust. 'Listen to me when I speak to you!' I pant. I am beside myself with anger. Water ebbs from the kettle on to the mattress. He backs through the doorway and sprawls over the threshold. Dazzled by the sun he curls again on his side in the dust.

'Where is the bottle? Tell me! Where is the brandy? Where did you get the brandy?' I stand over him with the broom, glad on the whole that no one is watching us, a grown man, a grown woman.

'Let me alone, miss! I didn't steal anything!'

'Where did you get the brandy?'

'The baas gave it to me, miss! I don't steal.'

'Get up and listen to me. The baas has had an accident. Do you understand? You must come and help.'

'Yes, miss.'

He struggles to his feet, wavers, staggers, and falls. I lift the broom high. He raises a leg resentfully in defence.

'Come on, for God's sake get a move on,' I scream, 'the baas will die if you don't help, and then it won't be my fault!'

'Just wait a moment, miss, it isn't easy.'

He makes no effort to rise. Lying on the ground he breaks into a smile.

'You sot, you filthy sot, you're finished here, I swear it! Pack your things and get out! I don't want to see you here again.' The broomhandle thuds against the sole of his shoe and spins out of my hands.

129. I am panting and toiling through the riverbed again. Would that the river came roaring down in flood and washed us away, sheep and all, leaving the earth clean! Perhaps that is

how the tale will end, if the house does not burn down first. But the last of the dawn mauve has been scorched away, we are in for yet another fine day, I would say that the sky is pitiless if I did not know that the sky is merely clear, the earth merely dry, the rocks merely hard. What purgatory to live in this insentient universe where everything but me is merely itself! I alone, the one speck not spinning blindly along but trying to create a life for itself amid this storm of matter, these bodies driven by appetite, this rural idiocy! My gorge rises, I am not used to running, I fart heavily in mid-stride. I should have lived in the city; greed, there is a vice I can understand. In the city I would have room to expand; perhaps it is not too late, perhaps I can still run away to the city disguised as a man, a wizened beardless little man, to practise greed and make my fortune and find happiness, though the last is not likely.

130. I stand heaving at the bedroom window. 'Hendrik is not coming. He is drunk. Daddy should not have given him brandy, he is not used to the stuff.'

The rifle from last night lies on the floor near the window.

His face is a liverish yellow. He sits as before clutching the curtain to him. He does not turn his head. There is no telling whether he has heard me.

131. I kneel over him. He is looking at the blank wall, but his gaze is focussed somewhere beyond it, on infinity perhaps, or even on his redeemer. Is he dead? Despite all the smallpox and influenza in my life I have never seen anything larger than a pig die.

His breath strikes my nostrils, feverish, foul.

'Water,' he whispers.

There are midges floating in the water-bucket. I scoop them off and drink a beakerful. Then I bring the full beaker back and hold it to his lips. He swallows it with reassuring energy.

'Can I help Daddy to get into bed?'

He is moaning to himself, gritting his teeth, one moan to

each shallow breath. His toes, sticking out from under the curtain, curl and uncurl.

'Help me,' he whispers, 'get the doctor quickly.' Tears roll down his cheeks.

I straddle him and, gripping him under the armpits, try to raise him. He gives me no help at all.

He is crying like a baby.

'Help me, help me, the pain is terrible! Quickly, get something to stop the pain!'

'There is no more brandy. Daddy gave it all to Hendrik; now that we need it there isn't any.'

'Help me, child, I can't bear it, I have never had such pain!'

132. My soles stick unpleasantly to the floor. I tramp about the house without plan or purpose, leaving marks which I shall have to clean.

He is sitting in a pool of blood like a baby that has wet itself.

133. A third time I cross the riverbed, trudging now, tired, fed up. I have the rifle slung over my shoulder. The butt bumps against my calves. I feel like an old campaigner, but wonder what I look like.

Hendrik is lying flat on his back snoring. Another stinking man.

'Hendrik, get up at once or I shoot. I am sick of your games. The baas needs you.'

When one truly means what one says, when one speaks not in shouts of panic, but quietly, deliberately, decisively, then one is understood and obeyed. How pleasing to have identified a universal truth. Hendrik gets groggily to his feet and follows me. I give him the rifle to carry. The cartridge in the breech is spent and has been since before midnight. I am harmless, despite appearances.

134. 'Hendrik, get him under the shoulders, then we can lift him on to the bed.'

With Hendrik at the shoulders and myself at the knees we lift my father on to the tousled bed. He is groaning and talking to himself in delirium. I fetch a basin of water, a sponge, carbolic acid.

What I have not seen is the gaping wound in his back from which blood seeps steadily. Petals of flesh stand out from it. I wash delicately around them. When the sponge touches raw flesh he jerks. But at least the bullet is out.

There is not enough bandage for a wound of this size. With dressmaking shears I begin to cut a sheet into strips. It takes a long time. Hendrik fidgets until I tell him to wave the flies off his master. He does so self-consciously.

While Hendrik raises the torso I cover the two holes with wads of lint and wind the bandage round and round the thick waist. The sex is smaller than I thought it would be, almost lost in a bush of black hair straggling up to the navel: a pale boy, a midget, a dwarf, an idiot son who, having survived for years shut away in the cellar, tasting only bread and water, talking to the spiders, singing to himself, is one night dressed in new clothes, set free, made much of, pampered, feasted, and then executed. Poor little thing. It is not possible to believe I came from there, or from whatever that puffy mass is below it. If I were told that I am an idea my father had many years ago and then, bored with it, forgot, I would be less incredulous, though still sceptical. I am better explained as an idea I myself had, also many years ago, and have been unable to shake off.

Hendrik is embarrassed by my diligent hands and eyes, my dutiful hands and eyes, but all the same my woman's hands and eyes wandering so near this pale unprotected manhood. I am aware of his embarrassment, and turn and smile the first frank smile I have given him today, or perhaps in all the years I have known him. He lowers his eyes. Can brown-skinned people blush?

Over my father's head I draw a clean nightshirt. With Hendrik's help I roll it down over his knees. Now he is clean and decent.

'Now we can only wait and see, Hendrik. Go to the kitchen, I will come and make coffee in a moment.'

135. So all of a sudden here I am at the centre of a field of moral tensions, they are no less, for which my upbringing has barely prepared me. What am I going to do? When he finds his balance Hendrik will want to know whether the accident is an eccentricity of the ruling caste or whether I am culpable and can be exploited. He will want to know who is most shamed, he or I, we or they, and who will pay more for silence. Klein-Anna, if she can ever be found, will want to know whether I am angered or frightened by her liaison with my father. She will want to know whether I am prepared to protect her from Hendrik and whether in future I will try to keep her away from my father. Jointly she and Hendrik will want to know whether they must leave the farm or whether the scandal is to be hushed up. My father will want to know what penitence I can be made to do; whether I will work upon the girl while he is out of the way; whether a fiction is to be brought into being among the four of us to explain his injury, a hunting accident, for example. I will be watched by hooded eyes, my every word will be weighed, words will be spoken to me whose bland taste, whose neutral colour, whose opaque surface will fail to cover nuances of derision. Smiles will pass behind my back. A crime has been committed. There must be a criminal. Who is the guilty one? I am at a terrible disadvantage. Forces within me belonging to the psychology I so abhor will take possession of me and drive me to believe that I willed the crime, that I desired by father's death. With the dark subtle figures of Hendrik and Klein-Anna wagging their fingers behind me I shall find my days turned into a round of penitence. I shall find myself licking my father's wounds, bathing Klein-Anna and bringing her to his bed, serving Hendrik hand and foot. In the dark before dawn, drudgemaiden of a drudge-maiden, I shall stoke the fire. I shall serve them breakfast in bed

and bless them when they revile me. Already the snake has come and the old Eden is dead!

136. I deceive myself. It is worse than that, far worse. He will never get well. What was once pastoral has become one of those stifling stories in which brother and sister, wife and daughter and concubine prowl and snarl around the bedside listening for the death-rattle, or stalk each other through the dim passages of the ancestral home. It is not fair! Born into a vacuum in time, I have no understanding of changing forms. My talent is all for immanence, for the fire or ice of identity at the heart of things. Lyric is my medium, not chronicle. As I stand in this room I see not father and master dying on the bed but the sunlight reflected with unholy brilliance from his beaded forehead; I smell the odour that blood has in common with stone, with oil, with iron, the odour that folk travelling through space and time, inhaling and exhaling the black, the empty, the infinite, smell as they pass through the orbits of the dead planets, Pluto, Neptune, and those not yet discovered, so tiny are they and so remote, the odour that matter gives off when it is very old and wants to sleep. Oh father, father, if I could only learn your secrets, creep through the honeycomb of your bones, listen to the turmoil of your marrow, the singing of your nerves, float on the tide of your blood, and come at last to the quiet sea where my countless brothers and sisters swim, flicking their tails, smiling, whispering to me of a life to come! I want a second chance! Let me annihilate myself in you and come forth a second time clean and new, a sweet fish, a pretty baby, a laughing infant, a happy child, a gay girl, a blushing bride, a loving wife, a gentle mother in a story with beginning and end in a country town with kind neighbours, a cat on the doormat, geraniums on the windowledge, a tolerant sun! I was all a mistake! There was a black fish swimming among all those white fish and that black fish was chosen to be me. I was sister to none of them, I was ill chance itself, I was a shark, an infant black shark. Why did you not recognize it and cut its throat?

What kind of merciful father were you who never cared for me but sent me out into the world a monster? Crush me, devour me, annihilate me before it is too late! Wipe me clean, wipe out too these whispering watchers and this house in the middle of nowhere, and let me try again in a civilized setting! Wake up and embrace me! Show me your heart just once and I swear I will never look again, into your heart or any other, be it the heart of the meanest stone! I will give up this kind of talk too, every word of it! When the words come I will set fire to them! Do you not see that it is only despair, love and despair, that makes me talk this way? Speak to me! Do I have to call on you in words of blood to make you speak? What horrors more do you demand of me? Must I carve out my beseechings with a knife on your flesh? Do you think you can die before you have said Yes to me? Do you think I cannot breathe the breath of your lungs for you or pump your heart in my fist? Do you think I will lay pennies on your eyes before you have looked at me or tie up your jaw before you have spoken? You and I will live together in this room till I have my way, till the crack of doom, till the stars fall out of the sky. *I am I*! I can wait!

137. There is no change in his condition.

I am losing patience with everything. I have no stomach for trotting from room to room performing realistic tasks, conducting stupid conversation with Hendrik. Nothing happens or can be made to happen. We are in the doldrums. I twiddle my thumbs and fret. If only it would rain! If only lightning would strike and set the veld on fire! If only the last of the great reptiles would rise out of the slime at the bottom of the dam! If only naked men on ponies would come pouring out of the hills and massacre us! What must I do to save myself from the tedium of existence on this of all days? Why does Hendrik not plunge a breadknife into the breast of the man who wasted the joy of his life? Why does Klein-Anna not come out of her bolting-hole, wherever that is, and kneel before her husband and beg forgiveness and be cuffed and spat on and reconciled? Why is she not weeping at her paramour's bedside? Why is Hendrik so withdrawn? Why, instead of waiting tirelessly in the kitchen, is he not hovering about me, smiling secret smiles and hinting at the price of silence? Why does my father not rouse himself and curse us? Why is it left to me to give life not only to myself, minute after surly minute, but to everyone else on the farm, and the farm itself, every stick and stone of it? I said once that I slept, but that was a lie. I said that every night I donned my white nightdress and fell asleep with my horny toes pointing to the stars. But that cannot be true. How can I afford to sleep? If for one moment I were to lose my grip on the world, it would fall apart: Hendrik and his shy bride would dissolve to dust in each other's arms and sift to the floor, the crickets would stop chirping, the house would deliquesce to a pale abstract of lines and angles against a pale sky, my father would float like a black cloud and be sucked into the lair inside my head to beat the walls and roar like a bear. All that would remain would be me, lying for that fatal instant in a posture of sleep on an immaterial bed above an immaterial earth before everything vanished. I make it all up in order that it shall make me up. I cannot stop now.

138. But I have dreams. I do not sleep but I have dreams: how I manage that I do not know. One of my dreams is about a bush. When the sun has set and the moon is dark and the stars shed so little light that one cannot see a hand in front of one's face, the bush I dream of glows with an unearthly light. I stand before the bush watching it, and the bush watches me back through the depths of profoundest night. Then I grow sleepy. I yawn and lie down and sleep, in my sleep, and the last star goes out in the sky above me. But the bush, alone in the universe, but for me who am now asleep and therefore who knows where, continues to shed on me its radiance.

Such is my dream about the burning bush. There is a scheme of interpretation, I am sure, according to which my dream about the bush is a dream about my father. But who is to say what a dream about my father is?

139. 'Must I harness the donkeys, miss?'
   'No, let us wait, it will only make the pain worse if we move the baas now.'

140. The girl is in the sewing-room. She must have hidden here all night, crouching in a corner, listening to the groans from the bedroom and the footfalls on the gravel outside, until she fell asleep on the floor in a nest of drapery like a cat. Having decided to find her, I have found her at once: one does not grow up in a house without learning the nuances of its breathing.
   'Well, now the fun and games are over! And where are your clothes? Leave my blankets alone, please, you have clothes of your own. Well, come on, what are you going to do now? What are you going to say to your husband? What are you going to say to him about last night? Come on, speak up, what are you going to tell your husband? What have you been up to here in the house? You slut! You filth! Look what a mess you've caused! It's your fault, all this mess is your fault! But one thing I tell you, you get out today, you and Hendrik, I am finished with you! And stop crying, it's too late to cry, you should rather have cried yesterday, it won't help today! Where are your clothes? Put your clothes on, don't stand naked in front of me, put your clothes on and get out, I don't want to see you again! I'm going to tell Hendrik to come and fetch you.'
   'Please, miss, my clothes are gone.'
   'Don't lie to me, your clothes are in the bedroom where you were!'
   'Yes, miss. Please, miss, he will hit me.'
   Thus, venting torrents of mean-spirited resentment on the girl, swelling with ire and self-righteousness, do I become for a blessed interval a woman among women, shrew among doughty country shrews. It comes of itself, one needs no lessons, only meek folk around one and a grudge against them for not

80

speaking back. I am cantankerous, but only because there is infinite space around me, and time before and after from which history seems to have retreated, and evidence in these bowed faces of limitless power. Everywhere I beat my fists on air. What is there for me but dreary expansion to the limits of the universe? Is it any wonder that nothing is safe from me, that the lowliest veld-flower is likely to find itself raped in its being or that I should dream with yearning of a bush that resists my metaphysical conquest? Poor Hendrik, poor Anna, what chance have they?

141. 'Hendrik! Listen carefully. Anna is in the house. She is sorry about everything that has happened. She says it won't happen again. She wants to ask your forgiveness. What I want to know is: must I send her out, or is there going to be trouble? Because, Hendrik, I am telling you here and now, if you give trouble I wash my hands of both of you, you can get out today. I want to make myself quite clear. What happens between you and Anna is none of my business; but if she comes to me and says you have been cruel to her, beware!

'Anna! Come here at once! Come on, hurry up, he won't do anything!'

The child shuffles out. She is wearing her own clothes again, the brown frock to her knees, the blue cardigan, the scarlet kerchief. She stands in front of Hendrik tracing patterns with her big toe in the gravel. Her face is blotched with tear-stains. She sniffs and sniffs.

Hendrik speaks.

'Miss must not get upset, but miss is interfering too much.'

He moves a step closer to Klein-Anna. His voice is big with passion as I have never heard it before. Anna slides behind me, wiping her nose on her sleeve. It is a beautiful morning and I am caught in a dogfight. 'You! I'll kill you!' says Hendrik. Anna grips my dress between my shoulderblades. I shake myself loose. Hendrik swears at her in words whose meaning I can mostly only guess at, I have not heard them before, how surprising.

81

'Stop it!' I scream. Ignoring me he lunges at Anna. At once she spins on her heel and starts running; and he after her. She is nimble and barefoot, he shod but driven by fury. Shrieking without letup she spins leftward and rightward trying to throw him off. Then, in the middle of the schoolhouse road a hundred yards from where I stand, she suddenly falls and curls into a cringing ball. Hendrik begins to punch and kick; she screams despairingly. I pick up my skirts and run towards them. This is certainly action, and unambiguous action too. I cannot deny that there is exhilaration mixed in with my alarm.

142. Hendrik is kicking rhythmically at her with his soft shoes. He does not look up at me, his face is wet with sweat, he has work to do. If there were a stick to hand he would be using it, but there are not many sticks in this part of the world, his wife is fortunate.

I tug at his waistcoat. 'Leave her!' I say. It is as if he expected me, for he takes hold of my wrist, then, turning smoothly, of the other wrist too. For a second he stands face to face with me clenching my wrists against his chest. I smell his heat, not without distaste. 'Stop it!' I say. 'Let me go!'

A number of movements follow which, in the flurry of the moment, I cannot discriminate, though I shall be able to do so later in the cool of retrospection, I am sure. I am shaken back and forth: my feet stagger one way and another out of time with my body, my head jerks, I am off balance yet not allowed to fall. I know I look ridiculous. Happily, living here in the heart of nowhere, one need not keep up a front for anyone, not even, it would now appear, for the servants. I am not angry, though my teeth rattle: there are worse things than standing up for the weak, there are worse things than being shaken, not unkindly, I can feel no malevolence in this man whose passion is forgivable and whose eyes are anyhow, I see, closed.

I stumble backward, let go by Hendrik, who turns away from me to the girl, who is gone. I fall heavily on my backside, my palms are scorched by the gravel, my skirts fly in the air, I am dizzy but gay and ready for more, perhaps what has been wrong all these years is simply that I have had no one to play with. The blood thuds in my ears. I close my eyes: in a moment I will be myself.

143. Hendrik is out of sight. I beat my clothes and the dust rises in clouds. The pocket of my skirt is ripped clear off and the keyring with the keys to the storehouse, the pantry, and the dining-room cabinets is gone. I scratch around until I find it, pat my hair straight, and set off up the schoolhouse road after Hendrik. Event has been following event, yet the exhilaration is fading, I am losing momentum, I am not sure why I follow them further, perhaps they ought to be left to settle their debts and make peace in their own way. But I do not want to be alone, I do not want to begin moping.

144. Hendrik crouches on hands and knees over the girl on the truckle bed as if about to sink his teeth into her throat. She lifts her knees to push him off; her dress falls back over her hips. 'No,' she pleads with him, and I hear it all, stopping suddenly in the schoolhouse doorway, catching first the highlights on her thighs and his cheekbones, then, as my eyes adjust to the gloom inside, everything else – 'No, not here, she'll catch us!'

The two heads turn in unison to the shape in the doorway. 'God!' she says. She drops her legs, clutches her skirt down, and turns her face to the wall. Hendrik comes upright on his knees. He grins straight at me. From his middle juts out unhidden what must be his organ, but grotesquely larger than it should be, unless I am mistaken. He says: 'Miss has surely come to watch.'

145. I open the sickroom door and am hit by the sweet stench. The room is peaceful and sunny but filled with a high complex drone. There are hundreds of flies here, common houseflies and the larger green-tailed blowflies whose curt rasp is submerged

83

in the general hum so that the texture of sound in the room is replete and polyphonal.

My father's eye is upon me. His lips form a word which I cannot hear. I stand in the doorway unwilling. I should not have come back. Behind every door there is a new horror.

The word comes again. I tiptoe to the bedside. The pitch of the buzzing rises as the flies make way before me. One fly continues to sit on the bridge of his nose and clean its face. I brush it away. It rises, circles, and settles on my forearm. I brush it away. I could spend all day like this. The hum grows steady again.

Water is the word he is saying. I nod.

I raise the bedclothes and look. He is lying in a sea of blood and shit that has already begun to cake. I tuck the bedclothes back under his armpits.

'Yes, daddy,' I say.

146. I hold the beaker to his lips and he sucks noisily.

'More,' he whispers.

'First wait a little,' I tell him.

'More.'

He drinks more water and grips my arm, waiting for something, listening for something far away. I wave the flies off. He begins to croon, more and more loudly, his whole body stiffening. I should be doing something for his pain. The pressure on my arm is forcing me down. I yield, crouching at the bedside, not wishing to sit on the ooze in the bed. The stench grows sickening.

'Poor daddy,' I whisper, and put a hand on his forehead. He is hot.

Under the bedclothes there is a liquid convulsion. He releases his breath with a gasp. I cannot stand this. One by one I pick the fingers from my arm, but one by one they close again. He is by no means without strength. I wrench my arm loose and stand up. His eyes open. 'The doctor will soon be here,' I tell him. The mattress is irrecoverable, it will have to be burned. I must close the window. I must also put back the curtains, the afternoon heat and the stench together will be too much for anyone. I will not stand for any more flies.

147. The flies, which ought to be in transports of joy, sound merely cross. Nothing seems to be good enough for them. For miles around they have forsaken the meagre droppings of the herbivores and flown like arrows to this gory festival. Why are they not singing? But perhaps what I take for petulance is the sound of insect ecstasy. Perhaps their lives from cradle to grave, so to speak, are one long ecstasy, which I mistake. Perhaps the lives of animals too are one long ecstasy interrupted only at the moment when they know with full knowledge that the knife has found their secret and they will never again see the goodly sun which even at this instant goes black before them. Perhaps the lives of Hendrik and Klein-Anna are ecstasy, if not acute ecstasy then at least a kind of gentle streaming of radiance from eyes and fingertips which I do not see, interrupted only on such occasions as last night and this morning. Perhaps ecstasy is not after all so rare. Perhaps if I talked less and gave myself more to sensation I would know more of ecstasy. Perhaps, on the other hand, if I stopped talking I would fall into panic, losing my hold on the world I know best. It strikes me that I am faced with a choice that flies do not have to make.

148. One after another the flies fall under my swatter, some erupting in gouts of crop-slime, some folding their legs and passing neatly away, some spinning about angrily on their backs until the *coup de grâce* descends. The survivors circle the room waiting for me to tire. But I must keep a clean house and to that end I am tireless. If I abandon this room, locking the door, stuffing the cracks with rags, I will in time find myself abandoning another room, and then others, until the house is all but lost, its builders all but betrayed, the roof sagging, the shutters clapping, the woodwork cracking, the fabrics rotting,

85

the mice having a field day, only a last room intact, a single room and a dark passage where I wander night and day tapping at the walls, trying for old times' sake to remember the various rooms, the guest-room, the dining-room, the pantry in which the various jams wait patiently, sealed under candlewax, for a day of resurrection that will never come; and then retire, dizzy with sleepiness, for even mad old women, insensible to heat and cold, taking their nourishment from the passing air, from motes of dust and drifting strands of spiderweb and fleas' eggs, must sleep, to the last room, my own room, with the bed against the wall and the mirror and the table in the corner where, chin in hand, I think my mad old woman's thoughts and where I shall die, seated, and rot, and where the flies will suck at me, day after day after day, to say nothing of the mice and the ants, until I am a clean white skeleton with nothing more to give the world and can be left in peace, with the spiders in my eyesockets spinning traps for the stragglers to the feast.

149. A day must have intervened here. Where there is a blank there must have been a day during which my father sickened irrecoverably, and during which Hendrik and Klein-Anna made their peace, for thenceforth they were as before, or if not as before then changed toward the wiser and sadder in ways I could not discern. It must have been a day which I passed somehow. Perhaps I spent it asleep. Perhaps, having killed all the the flies, I fetched a wet sponge and cooled my father's brow until I could no longer tolerate the stench. Perhaps I went and stood in the passage waiting for his call, and there fell asleep and dreamed of rain and the veld covered in flowers, white and violet and orange, rippling in the wind, till at nightfall I awoke and arose to feed the chickens. Perhaps then, in the gloom, with the feed-bowl under my arm. I stood listening to the night breeze rustle the leaves, and watched the bats flicker against the last light, and felt the sweeping melancholy of those who pass their days in the midst of insupportable beauty in the

knowledge that one day they will die. Perhaps I prayed then, not for the first time, that I would die tranquil and not begrudge myself to the earth, but look forward to life as a flower or as the merest speck in the gut of a worm, unknowing. I think it is possible that such a day did intervene, and that I did spend it like that, helpless in the face of my father's pain, wishing it away, dozing, wandering about in the yard in the cool of the evening thinking how it would be when we were all gone. There are, however, other ways in which I could have spent the day and which I cannot ignore. I could have been the one who tried to help him out of bed and failed, he being heavy, I being slight. This would explain how he came to die so hideously draped over the edge of the bed, his face purple, his eyes bulging, his tongue hanging out. Perhaps I wanted to move him out of the morass he lay in. Perhaps I wanted to take him to another room. Perhaps, dismayed and sickened, I abandoned him. Perhaps I cradled his head in my arms and sobbed, saying, 'Daddy, please help me, I can't do it by myself.' Perhaps when it grew clear that he could not help, that he had no strength, that he was preoccupied above all else with what was happening inside him, perhaps then I said, 'Daddy, forgive me, I didn't mean it, I loved you, that was why I did it.'

150. But, to tell the truth, I am wary of all these suppositions. I suspect that the day the day was missing I was not there; and if that is so I shall never know how the day was filled. For I seem to exist more and more intermittently. Whole hours, whole afternoons go missing. I seem to have grown impatient with the sluggish flow of time. Once I would have been content to fill my days with musings; but now, having been through a carnival of incident, I am quite seduced. Like the daughters in the boarding-houses I sit tapping my fingernails on the furniture, listening to the tick of the clock, waiting for the next thing to happen. Once I lived in time as a fish in water, breathing it, drinking it, sustained by it. Now I kill time and time kills me. Country ways! How I long for country ways.

151. I sit at the kitchen table waiting for my coffee to cool. Hendrik and Klein-Anna stand over me. They say that they are waiting to hear what to do, but I cannot help them. There is nothing to do in the kitchen since no one eats meals any more. What there is to be done on the farm Hendrik knows better than I. He must preserve the sheep from jackals and wildcats. He must annihilate the ticks and the blowfly grubs. He must help the ewes to lamb. He must make the garden grow and save it from the army worm. Therefore it is not true that Hendrik and Klein-Anna are here waiting for orders: they are waiting to see what I will do next.

152. I sit at the kitchen table waiting for my coffee to cool. Over me stand Hendrik and Klein-Anna.

'The smell is getting bad,' says Hendrik.

'Yes, we will have to make a fire,' I reply.

I am thankful, in times of trouble, to have a trusty helper. Hendrik's eyes meet mine. We see the same purpose. I smile, and he smiles too, a sudden unambiguous smile that shows his stained teeth and his pink gums.

153. Hendrik explains to me how the entire windowframe can be lifted from the wall. He shows me first how the plaster can be chipped away to reveal the bolts securing the frame to the wall. He shows me how these bolts can be sawn through with a hacksaw blade. He saws through the four bolts, dust and filings falling in pyramids at our feet. He forces out the frame, the sashes still latched together within it, and puts it aside. He explains how the windowledge is levelled before the first bricks are laid. He lays eighteen courses of bricks and plasters them over. I wash the trowel and the hod for him. I scrub the lime from under his fingernails with vinegar. All night and all day we wait for the plaster to dry. Anna brings us coffee. We whitewash the new plaster. We burn the windowframe. The glass cracks in the flames. We grind it to powder under our heels.

154. Hendrik and I climb the stairs to the loft. In the close heat he shows me how to paint the floor with tar so that the cracks between the boards are sealed. I tend the fire under the tarbucket while he paints. On hands and knees we back out of the loft.

155. Hendrik removes the doorknob and shows me how to stuff caulking into the cracks with a blunt chisel. He lays sixteen courses of bricks to seal the doorway. I mix the mortar, I wash the tools, I scrub his fingernails. We strip off the old wallpaper and re-cover the passage with paper we have found in the loft. The old doorframe bulges, but we ignore it.

156. Hendrik shows me how to saw through bricks and mortar. We use the ripsaw that hangs in the stable. The teeth of this saw never grow blunt. We saw through the walls that hold the bedroom to the house. Our arms grow tired but we do not pause. I learn to spit on my hands before I grip the saw. Our labour brings us together. No longer is labour Hendrik's prerogative. I am his equal though I am the weaker. Klein-Anna climbs the ladder to bring us mugs of coffee and slices of bread and jam. We crawl under the house to saw through the foundations. Our honest sweat flows together in the dark warmth. We are like two termites. In perseverance lies our strength. We saw through the roof and through the floor. We shove the room off. Slowly it rises into the air, a ship of odd angles sailing black against the stars. Into the night, into empty space it floats, clumsily, since it has no keel. We stand in the dust and mice droppings, on ground where no sun has shone, watching it.

157. We pick up the body and carry it to the bathroom, Hendrik taking the shoulders, I the legs. We strip off the nightshirt and unwind the bandages. We seat the body in the bath and pour bucket after bucket of water over it. The water discolours and strings of excrement begin to float to the

surface. The arms hang over the sides of the bath, the mouth gapes, the eyes stare. After half an hour's soaking we clean the clotted hindparts. We bind the jaw and sew the eyes to.

158. On the hillside behind the house Hendrik piles brushwood and sets fire to it. We throw the nightclothes, the bandages, the bedclothes, and the mattress on to the flames. They smoulder through the afternoon, filling the air with the smell of burnt coir and feathers.

159. I sweep out all the dead flies and scrub with sand and soap until the bloodstains are only pale rose patches on the brown of the floorboards.

160. We carry the great bed to the stable, all three of us, and hoist it, one corner at a time, to the rafters, where we chain it fast against the day when it may again be needed.

161. From the loft we bring down an empty kist and into it pack the deceased's belongings, the Sunday suit, the black boots, the starched shirts, the wedding ring, the daguerrotypes, the diaries, the ledgers, the bundle of letters tied with a red ribbon. I read one of the letters aloud to Hendrik: 'How I long for you these days . . .' Hendrik follows my finger as I point out the words. He scrutinizes the family groups and picks me out unerringly among the other children, the brothers and sisters and half-brothers and half-sisters who perished in the various epidemics or went to the city to make their fortune and were never heard of again. The pictures show me tight-lipped and surly, but Hendrik does not mind. When we have finished we pack the papers away and padlock the chest and carry it up to the loft to await the resurrection.

162. We fold the green curtains away in a drawer and make new curtains of a gay floral material we have chanced on in the loft. Hendrik sits watching while my busy feet work the treadle

and my nimble fingers guide the seams. We hang our new curtains which make the room cool yet light. We smile at our enterprise. Klein-Anna brings coffee.

163. Hendrik and Klein-Anna stand over me waiting for instructions. I swirl the grounds in my coffee-cup. It is going to be a difficult day, I tell them, a day for waiting. Words come reluctantly to me, they clatter in my mouth and tumble out heavily like stones. Hendrik and Klein-Anna wait patiently. There are clouds massing to the north, I tell them, perhaps it is going to rain, perhaps in a few days the veld will be tipped with new green, the withered bushes shooting, the locusts, dormant all winter, now nosing their way out of the soil and hopping off in search of food attended by swarms of birds. We must beware in general, I tell them, of the revival of insect life that attends the rains and the efflorescence of the veld. I mention plagues of caterpillars. The birds are our allies, I tell them, the birds and the wasps, for wasps are predators too. Hendrik listens to me hat in hand, watching not my eyes but these lips of mine which I must wrestle into place over every syllable. The lips are tired, I explain to him, they want to rest, they are tired of all the articulating they have had to do since they were babies, since it was revealed to them that there was a law, that they could no longer simply part themselves to make way for the long *aaaa* which has, if truth be told, always been enough for them, enough of an expression of whatever this is that needs to be expressed, or clench themselves over the long satisfying silence into which I shall still, I promise, one day retire. I am exhausted by obedience to this law, I try to say, whose mark lies on me in the spaces between the words, the spaces or the pauses, and in the articulations that set up the war of sounds, the *b* against the *d*, the *m* against the *n*, and so forth, as well as in other places which I would be too weary to set out for you even if I felt that you understood, which I doubt, since you do not so much as know the alphabet. The law has gripped my throat, I say and do not say, it invades my larynx, its one hand

on my tongue, its other hand on my lips. How can I say, I say, that these are not the eyes of the law that stare from behind my eyes, or that the mind of the law does not occupy my skull, leaving me only enough intellection to utter these doubting words, if it is I uttering them, and see their fallaciousness? How can I say that the law does not stand fullgrown inside my shell, its feet in my feet, its hands in my hands, its sex drooping through my hole; or that when I have had my chance to make this utterance, the lips and teeth of the law will not begin to gnaw their way out of this shell, until there it stands before you, the law grinning and triumphant again, its soft skin hardening in the air, while I lie sloughed, crumpled, abandoned on the floor?

164. We stand in the dim passage before the one door that, as far back in time as I can remember, has always stood locked. What do you keep in the locked room? I used to ask my father. There is nothing in it, he used to reply, it is a junkroom, there is nothing but broken furniture, and besides, the key is lost. Now I tell Hendrik to open the door. With a chisel he prises the socket of the lock loose. Then he batters the door with his four-pound hammer until the jamb splinters and it springs open. From the floor rises a cloud of fine dust. There is a smell of cold tired bricks. Klein-Anna brings a lamp. In the far corner we see twelve cane-bottomed chairs piled neatly. We see a wardrobe, a narrow bed, a wash-stand with a pitcher and basin on it. The bed is neatly made up. I pat it and dust rises from the grey pillows, the grey sheets. Everywhere are cobwebs. They have made a room without a window, I say to Hendrik.

165. The wardrobe is locked. Hendrik springs the lock with his knife. It is full of clothes, the sad noble clothes of bygone times that I would love to wear. I lift out a dress, white, with full sleeves and high collar, and hold it up against Klein-Anna. She puts the lamp down on the floor and smooths the dress against her body. I help her to undress. I take her old clothes

from her and fold them on the bed. She lowers her eyes. The light glows on her bronze flanks and breasts for which I find again I have no words. My heart quickens as I settle the dress over her head and fasten the buttons against her spine. She wears no underclothes.

166. Though the shoes are all too narrow for her, Klein-Anna insists on a pair. I slip them on, leaving the straps unbuttoned. Unsteadily she rises and totters. She leads us out of the room of surprises to the stoep. The sun is setting, the sky is a tumult of oranges and reds and violets. Up and down the stoep struts Klein-Anna mastering the shoes. If only we could eat our sunsets, I say, we would all be full. I stand side by side with Hendrik, watching. Hendrik has lost his old stiffness. His arm brushes my side. I do not flinch. It is not beyond reason that I should want to whisper something to him, something kindly and affectionate and amusing about Anna, that I should turn towards him, and he bend towards me, that I should for a brief moment find myself in the pocket of air that is his own private space, the space that, when he stands still, as now, he fills with his own breathing and his own smells, that I should find myself breathing in once, twice, as often as it takes to say what I have to say, Hendrik's own air, and find myself for the first time breathing it in with receptive nostrils, alive to the musk, the sweat, the smoke that once repelled me. This, after all, is how people smell in the country who have laboured honestly, sweating under the hot sun, cooking the food they have tilled or killed over fire they have made with their own hands. Perhaps, I tell myself, I too will come to smell like that if I can change my ways. I blush for my own thin smell, the smell of an unused woman, sharp with hysteria, like onions, like urine. How can he ever wish to burrow his nose in my armpit, as I mine in his!

167. Klein-Anna turns at the end of her promenade and smiles at us. I see no trace of jealousy. She knows how tight she holds

93

Hendrik. They sleep together as man and wife. They have connubial secrets. In the warm dark they lie in each other's arms and talk about me. Hendrik says amusing things and Anna giggles. He tells her about my lonely life, my solitary walks, the things that I do when I think no one is looking, the way I talk to myself, the way my arms jerk. He parodies my cross gabble. Then he tells her of my fear of him, the harsh words I speak to keep him at a distance, the odour of fright he can smell floating off me. He tells her what I do by myself in bed. He tells her how I roam the house by night. He tells her what I dream. He tells her what I need. He tells her that I need a man, that I need to be covered, to be turned into a woman. I am a child, he tells her, despite my years, I am an old child, a sinister old child full of stale juices. Someone should make a woman of me, he tells her, someone should make a hole in me to let the old juices run out. Should I be the one to do it, he asks her, to climb through the window one night and lie with her and make a woman of her and slip away before dawn? Do you think she would let me? Would she pretend it was a dream and let it happen, or would it be necessary to force her? Would I be able to fight my way in between those scraggy knees? Would she lose her head and scream? Would I have to hold her mouth shut? Would she not be as tight and dry and unrelenting to the last as leather? Would I force my way into that dusty hole only to be crushed to jelly in a vice of bone? Or is it possible that after all she would be soft, as a woman is soft, as you are soft, here? And Anna pants in the dark, cleaving to her man.

168. Klein-Anna turns at the end of her promenade and smiles at us. She is blithe, she knows all that I long for and she does not mind. I would like to stroll arm in arm with her of a Saturday night dressed in my gayest clothes, whispering and giggling like a girl, showing myself off to the country beaux. I would like to hear from her, in a quiet corner, the great secrets of life, how to be beautiful, how to win a husband, how to

please a man. I would like to be her little sister, I have had a late start in life, the years behind me are as if passed in slumber, I am still only an ignorant child. I would like to share a bed with her, and when she tiptoes in at midnight peep with one eye at her undressing, and sleep all night cuddled against her back.

169. 'I can't sleep alone tonight,' I tell them. 'The two of you must come and sleep in the house tonight.'

The words have come out without premeditation. I feel joy. That must be how other people speak, from their hearts.

'Come on, there is nothing to be afraid of, I assure you there are no ghosts.'

They search each other's eyes, weighing my motives, sending messages to each other through the dusk that I cannot detect. Hendrik has drawn away from me, I am out of his pocket of warmth. Does he feel out of his depth?

'No, miss,' he murmurs, 'I think we had better go home now.'

I grow stronger as he grows weaker.

'No: I want you to sleep here, just for the one night. Otherwise I am all alone in the house. We can make up a bed on a mat in the kitchen, it will be quite comfortable. Come along, Anna, come and help.'

170. Hendrik and Anna stand by their bed waiting for me to retire.

'Remember to blow out the light before you go to sleep,' I say, 'and Anna, please see to it that the fire is lit tomorrow morning. Goodnight, Hendrik, goodnight, Anna.' I am briskness itself.

'Goodnight, miss.'

171. When they have had time to settle I return and listen outside the closed door. I am barefoot: if the prowling scorpions want me let them have me. I hear nothing at all, not a stir, not

95

a whisper. If I am holding my breath then they are holding theirs. How can I hope to deceive them, countryfolk who can hear a hooffall a mile away through their soles and fingertips?

172. I lie on my bed and wait. The clock ticks, time passes, no one comes. I fall asleep and do not dream. The sun rises. I wake and dress. The kitchen is empty, the bedclothes are folded, the fire is lit.

173. I stride up the dust road past the three thorn-trees, across a corner of the lands, to the graveyard. One half of the grave-yard, set off by low white-painted railings, is for the dynasties who have farmed this land, buried now in the shale under their engraved slabs and scrolls. The other half is more densely packed with the tumuli of their shepherds and housemaids and the children of these. I walk among the stones until I come to the grave I have marked out, the grave of someone of whose coming and going I know nothing, to whom I owe no pious duty. By the weathered granite slab is the mouth of a tunnel going at an angle into the earth. In this dead man's bed a porcupine, perhaps by now also generations gone, hollowed out a home for itself and slept and raised its young.

174. Hendrik sits with his young wife on the bench in the shade of his cottage. It is Sunday.

'Hendrik, fetch a pick and spade and come with me to the graveyard, please. Anna, you had better stay here.'

175. Hendrik cannot budge the gravestone by himself. It is work for four men, he says. He chops the earth away around the three embedded edges but the stone sits fast.

'Chop the whole of this side loose. Make the hole wider, as wide as the entire length of the stone.'

'Miss, this is a porcupine hole, there's nothing in it.'

'Do as I tell you, Hendrik.'

Hendrik toils while I circle him. The grave has been filled

in with stone chips and soil, the strata are broken, it is not hard to dig, that is why the porcupine chose to live here, close to the lucerne fields.

Once Hendrik has widened the entrance tunnel we see, as I expected, the lair, a considerable rounded chamber, beyond. Though I lie on my belly and shade my eyes, the glare is too bright for me to see its back wall.

'How deep is the hole, Hendrik? Feel with the spade. I don't want to disturb the coffin.'

'No, miss, it's big but it doesn't go deep, porcupines don't burrow deep, they make a big chamber like this, just the one.'

'And what about a person, Hendrik – is that hole big enough to hold a person?'

'Yes, miss, it's big, a person can easily get into it.'

'Just to make sure, show me how a person gets in.'

'Me? No, miss, it's not yet time for me to climb into the grave!' He laughs but stands firm, tilting his hat back on his head.

176. I bundle my skirt around my knees and lower my legs into the hole. I push myself backward into the dark. Hendrik leans on his spade watching.

I am wholly inside. I try to stretch but cannot extend my legs.

I curl up in the cool earth and turn away from the light. My hair is full of dirt. I close my eyes the better to relish the dark. I search my heart and can find no reason to leave. I could make this my second home. I could get Hendrik to bring me food. I would not need much. At night I could crawl out to stretch my legs. Perhaps in time I would even learn to howl to the moon, to prowl around the sleeping farmhouse looking for scraps. I can find no reason to open my eyes again.

'Yes,' I tell Hendrik. My voice is thick, my words boom in my head. 'It's big enough. Help me out.' He leans down, watching the mouth of his mistress move in the shadow of the hole.

177. The body lies ready on the bathroom floor sewn into a grey tarpaulin. I have heard that seamen put the last stitch through the nose, to make sure, but I cannot bring myself to do so. I have not wept at my task. It is not that my heart is hard. There must be someone to wash the corpse, there must be someone to dig the grave.

178. I emerge on to the stoep and call in a strong steady voice: 'Hendrik!'

Hendrik rises from his spot of shade and crosses the yard.

'Hendrik, please fetch the wheelbarrow and put it at the kitchen door.'

'Yes, miss.'

When he comes to the back door I am waiting for him.

'Come and help me carry the body.'

He looks dubiously at me. This is the moment at which he baulks. I am ready for it.

'Hendrik, I want to speak frankly. We can't wait any longer. It is hot, the baas must be buried. There are only you and I who can do it. I can't do it by myself, and I don't want strangers interfering. This is a family matter, something private. Do you understand what I am saying?'

'What about a minister?' He is mumbling, he is uncertain, he will give no trouble.

'Come on, Hendrik, we have no time to waste. Help me carry it.'

I turn, he follows.

179. We lift the parcel, he at the head, I at the feet, and carry it through the house into the sunlight. There is no one to see us. There has never been anyone to see what goes on here. We are outside the law, therefore live only by the law we recognize in ourselves, going by our inner voice. My father reclines in his wheelbarrow, making a last tour of his domain. We trudge up the track to the graveyard, Hendrik pushing, I keeping the bundled legs from slipping sideways.

180. Hendrik will have nothing to do with the burying. 'No, miss,' he says again and again, backing away and shaking his head.

I push and pull until the barrow stands close to the hole. Given time I can do whatever a man can do. Gripping the ankles under my arm I strain to haul the bundle off. The barrow tips sideways, I jump back, and the body slides face-down to the ground. 'Don't just stand there, help me!' I scream. 'You damned *hotnot*, it's all your fault, you and your whore!' I am dizzy with rage. He turns, clamps his hat down on his head, and begins to march away. 'Filth! Coward!' I scream after him. With the gawky movements of a woman I throw a stone at him. It falls far short. He pays no heed.

181. The hips are too wide for the hole, the body will not slide in on its side and the bent knees cannot be straightened inside the tarpaulin. I must either widen the hole or break open the parcel. I hate destroying good handiwork. I have neither knife nor spade with me. I chop at the earth with a stone but it barely makes an impression. I should have tied up the tarpaulin with rope, this way I have no grip on it, my fingers are tired from clutching and pulling.

182. When I come back with the spade the flies are already here, rising in a cloud from the grey bundle and buzzing in the air, impatient for me to go away. I wave my arms about. It is late in the afternoon. How time passes when one is busy. The spade is of the wrong shape, it is meant for shovelling while I need something that will bite into the earth. I use the side of the blade to chop, every now and then striking sparks off the gravestone, showering myself with dirt, but finally widening the hole an inch or two.

Again the body slides in as far as the hips and sticks. I kneel and push at it with all my force. I sit beside it and kick with both heels together. It turns slightly and the hips slip through. I heave at the torso, rotating it further till the shoulders lie flat.

Now shoulders and head will pass through, but feet and knees refuse to slide further, for the floor of the burrow drops and then slopes upward again. The fault is not in the knees, I see, but in the spine, which will not flex. I struggle on and on in the crimson glory of the declining sun, kicking at the shoulders first from the right, then from the left, achieving nothing. I will have to haul it all out again, cut open the sailcloth, and tie the ankles against the thighs so as to shorten it. But will there be enough flexure at the knees? Will I have to cut the tendons in the knees? Burial is all a mistake. I should have burned the body with the mattress and the bed and gone for a long walk in the veld to escape the smell. I should have dug a new grave in the riverbed or in the garden where the soil is soft. I should have excavated one of the humbler tumuli, what difference does it make where he lies? If I intend to settle him in this grave there is no way to do so but to pull him in, to climb in first and pull him in after me. And I am exhausted. I do not see how I can finish before nightfall. All my life there has been enough time, more than enough time, too much time, I have panted for the breath of life in the thin medium of our time. Haste is foreign to me, I am repelled by the odour of panic I detect in my sweat. I am neither god nor beast, why do I have to do everything by myself, down to the very last things, why have I had to live this life without aid? I cannot find it in me to open the graveclothes and confront again the darkening cheesy flesh that sired me. But if I do not bury it now will I ever bury it? Perhaps I should simply go to bed and wait there day in, day out, with a pillow over my head, singing to myself, while the bag lies in the sun, the flies buzzing around it and the ants crawling in and out, until it bloats and bursts and runs in black fluids; and then wait on until its passion is complete, until it is simple bones and hair, the ants having taken everything worthwhile and gone elsewhere; and then, if the stitching has held, get out of bed at last and pick it up and sling it into the porcupine hole and be free of it.

183. The bundle, hauled out again, lies like a great grey larva at the graveside, and I, its tireless mother, instinct-driven, set again about stowing it in the safe place I have chosen, though for what hibernation, with what cell-food, toward what metamorphosis I do not know, unless it be as a great grey moth creaking through the dusk toward the lamplit farmhouse, blundering through the fleeing bats, sawing the air with its pinions, the death's-head burning bright in the fur between its shoulders, its mandibles, if moths have mandibles, opened wide for its prey. I send the head down first into the hole, but again, because the spine will not flex, the thighs cannot pass through. The hounds of logic are running me down.

184. Light thickens, the birds are settling to roost. If I stand still for a moment I can hear the clank of Hendrik's milk-pail. The cow lows for him. His wife waits by the hearth. In all this wide world there are only two creatures with no place to lay their heads.

185. I slip into the dark of the hole. The first stars are out. I grip the foot of the parcel, brace myself, and haul. The body slides in easily as far as the thighs. I lift the feet up off the ground and haul again. It slides in as far as the shoulders. The mouth of the hole is blocked, I am in pitch blackness. I lift the feet over my knee, embrace the parcel about the shoulders, and haul a third time. The head thuds in, the stars reappear, it is finished. I creep over the body and out into the free air. What a pity I have learned to name no more than the Southern Cross. I must rest, I cannot yet fill the hole in tonight, Hendrik will have to do it in the morning. He will have to wheel sand from the riverbed, there is no easier way, and pack the mouth with stones, and recompose the surface decently. I have done my part. Trembling with exhaustion I pick my way home.

186. All at once it is morning. It seems to lie in my power to

skip over whole days or nights as if they did not happen. In the empty kitchen I stretch and yawn.

Hendrik appears in the doorway. We greet each other decorously.

'Miss, I have come to ask – we haven't yet been paid.'

'Not yet paid?'

'No, miss, not yet paid.' He gives me his good smile, as though he has suddenly found a source of blinding joy in what we are saying. What has he to be happy about? Does he think I can return this friendliness? 'Look, miss, it's like this.' He approaches, he is going to explain, he does not see how I draw back. 'On Friday it was the first of the month. So on Monday we were supposed to get our money, all the people on the farm. But the baas didn't pay us. So we are still waiting, miss.'

'Didn't the baas give you anything at all?'

'No, miss, nothing, he gave us nothing of our money.'

'Yes, I know, but it isn't only money we are talking about. What about the brandy the baas gave you? And what about Klein-Anna? What about all those presents he gave her? They cost money, didn't they? The baas gave you all kinds of things, and yet on top of that you come and ask for money. Oh no! – for people like you I have no money.'

Trouble, always trouble! What do I know about money? Not in all my life have I had to touch a coin larger than a sixpence. Where am I going to lay my hands on money? Where did my father keep it? In a hole in his mattress, soaked in blood, burned by now to ashes? In a tobacco-tin under the floor? Under lock and key in the post office? How am I ever going to get hold of it? Did he make a will? Did he leave it to me or did he leave it to brothers and sisters and cousins I have never heard of? How will I ever find out? But do I want his money? Do I need money when I can live happily all my life on boiled pumpkin? And if I am too simple to need money, why does Hendrik need it? Why has he always to disappoint me?

'We did our work, miss.' The smile is quite gone, he is rigid with anger. 'Now we must get our money. The baas always paid us. Always.'

'Don't you stand there bandying words with me!' I have my own sources of anger. 'What work did you two really do? What work did that Anna of yours do? What work did you do yesterday afternoon when I had to bury the baas all by myself? Don't talk to me about work – I am the only one here who does any work! Go away, I haven't any money for you!'

'Right: if the miss says we must go then I suppose we must go!'

He is actually threatening me in sober daylight. He must have come, with his smile, to test me, to see what could be wrung from me, thinking that because I am alone and ridiculous I must also be weak and afraid. And now he is threatening me, thinking that I will be flustered.

'Listen carefully, Hendrik, and don't misunderstand me. I am not giving you money because I have no money. If you want to leave you can leave. But if you wait, I promise you will get your money, every penny you have earned. Now make up your mind.'

'No, miss, I understand. If miss says we must wait then we must wait, if miss promises us our money. Then we'll go ahead and take our slaughter-sheep.'

'Yes, take your sheep. But don't slaughter anything for the house until I tell you.'

'Yes, miss.'

187. The floor shines as it never shone when it was left to the care of servants. The doorknobs gleam, the windows sparkle, the furniture glows. Every last ray of light that enters the house is thrown from bright surface to bright surface endlessly. Every item of linen has been washed with my own hands, hung, ironed, folded, and packed away. My knees are tender from kneeling at the bathside, my hands raw from the scrubbing-board. My back aches, my head reels when I stand up. A smell of beeswax and linseed oil hangs in the air. The dust of ages,

the dust from on top of the wardrobes, the dust from the bedsprings, has been swept out of doors. The loft is spick and span. The chests stand in rows, packed tight with things I no longer need, their hasps and locks gleaming. My house has been set in order down to the last pin, and I have done it myself. Next comes the farm. One of these days, if they are not to stifle, the sheep must be shorn. If Hendrik refuses to do that task I will, my energies are boundless; I will put on my sunbonnet and go out with my sewing-scissors and catch the sheep by their hind legs and trap them between my knees and shear them one by one, day after day, until it is all done – let the wind take the wool, what good is it to me? Or perhaps I shall keep some of it to stuff a mattress with, so that I can lie on it at night, on all that oily warmth. If I cannot succeed in catching the sheep. Which is not unlikely (I have no sheepdog, dogs snarl and cower when I call them, they do not like me, it is the smell), then there is nothing for it, the sheep must perish, they must lie heaving and panting about the veld like filthy brown powderpuffs till their creator finds it in his heart to take them to himself. As for the windmills, the windmills will go on pumping day and night, they are faithful, they do not think, they do not mind the heat. The dams are overflowing. Hendrik still irrigates the lands, I see him in the evenings. When he ceases, out of boredom, out of pique, I will carry on. I need the fruit-trees and the vegetable garden. For the rest, the rye can die, the lucerne can die. The cow is drying up, the cow can die.

188. Between myself and them lies the dry river. They no longer come to the house, having no occasion. I have not paid them. Hendrik still milks the failing cow and irrigates the lands. Anna stays at home. Sometimes, from the stoep or from a window, I catch a glimpse of her scarlet kerchief bobbing about in the riverbed. On Friday evenings Hendrik comes to help himself to his coffee and sugar and meal and beans from the store. I watch him cross and re-cross the yard.

189. The fowls have gone wild, roosting in the trees. One by one they are being killed off by wildcats. A brood of chicks was lost last night. The feed is running out. I have not discovered any money. If it is in the post office then it is lost to me. But perhaps it really was burned up. Or perhaps there never was any money. Perhaps there will be no money unless I shear the sheep and sell their wool. In that case there will be no money.

190. This is no way to live.

191. Unable to sleep, I drift about the house at siesta time. I finger the strange clothes in the locked room. I look at myself in the mirror and try to smile. The face in the mirror smiles a haggard smile. Nothing has changed. I still do not like myself. Anna can wear these clothes but I cannot. From wearing black too long I have grown into a black person.

192. Hendrik is slaughtering a sheep a week. That is his way of claiming his due.

193. I get up in the mornings and look for things to clean. But things will not grow dirty fast enough. They are too little used, I must wait for the dust, and the dust falls in its own good time. I sulk; the house glitters.

194. Hendrik stands at the front door with his wife behind him.

'Miss, the coffee is finished, the flour is finished, almost everything is finished.'

'Yes, I know it's finished.'

'And miss still owes us.'

'I have no money. You don't work anyway, so why should I give you money?'

'Yes, but miss owes us, isn't that so?'

'It won't help to keep on asking, Hendrik, I am telling you I have no money.'

'Yes, but then miss can give us something else.'

195. I cannot carry on with these idiot dialogues. The language that should pass between myself and these people was subverted by my father and cannot be recovered. What passes between us now is a parody. I was born into a language of hierarchy, of distance and perspective. It was my father-tongue. I do not say it is the language my heart wants to speak, I feel too much the pathos of its distances, but it is all we have. I can believe there is a language lovers speak but cannot imagine how it goes. I have no words left to exchange whose value I trust. Hendrik is ducking and grinning secretly all the time he offers me the old locutions. 'Miss, miss, miss!' he says to my face; 'I know you, you are your father's daughter,' he says behind his hand; 'You are my wife's half-sister, where your father lay I lie too, I know that man, his mark is in my bed.' 'You, you, you,' sings Klein-Anna from behind him where I cannot see her.

196. Hendrik makes his appearance high above me on the platform outside the loft door dressed in the clothes of my father. It is grotesque! He postures, putting his hands on his hips and thrusting his chest out.

'*Aitsá!*' Klein-Anna calls up to him.

'Take off those clothes at once,' I cannot have this, he is going too far with me, 'I said you could take some of the baas's old clothes, but those clothes are not for you!'

He leers down at his wife, ignoring me.

'Hendrik!' I shout.

'*Hê!*' says Hendrik, holding out his arms and pirouetting on the platform. '*Aitsá!*' his wife calls back, dissolving in delighted laughter.

He has taken a white cotton shirt without collar, the best satin waistcoat, the twill trousers, even the good black boots. More shirts lie draped on the rails.

What can I do against the two of them? I am so alone, and a woman! I toil up the wooden stairs. This is my fate, I must go through with it.

The laughter has ceased. My eyes are level with his boots.

'Miss!' Is that finally hatred I hear in his voice? 'Miss, come on, tell old Hendrik: does miss want him to take off the baas's clothes?'

'I said you could take old clothes, Hendrik, but those clothes are not for you.' How many more of these cloddish words can I utter when my voice wants to wail and groan?

'Does miss want me to take the clothes off?'

I am trapped. I am going to cry. What more must I undergo before they will leave me alone?

Hendrik begins to unbuckle his trousers. I close my eyes and bow my head. I must be careful, if I try to go down the stairs backwards I will certainly slip and fall.

'Hey, look! Look, our miss, look!' What I hear in his voice is certainly hatred. Hot tears run down my cheeks though I pinch my eyes shut. Here is my punishment, it has come, it is now for me to bear it. 'Come on, don't be scared, our miss, it's only a man!'

So we stand in tableau for a long time.

'Stop now, you're hurting her.' Klein-Anna's voice comes up softly from below, saving me. I open my eyes and see her looking curiously straight into my face. She is a woman, therefore she is merciful. Is that a universal truth? Probing backwards one foot at a time I descend the steps and drag past her into the house. They are making an enemy of me, but why? Simply because I have no money for them?

197. They loiter about the yard in my parents' finery with no one to show it off to. These idle days tell on them as on me. We are all falling apart. Bored with each other, they have turned on me for sport. I pick up the rifle from its old place in the umbrella rack. Hendrik's back drifts into view above the front sight. What is Hendrik at this moment, a man plagued by ennui

sucking a grass-halm or a patch of white against green? Who can say? Gun and target slip into equilibrium and I pull the trigger. I am stunned and deafened, but I have been through this before, down to the ringing in my ears, I am an old hand. Anna is running like a child, flailing the air, stumbling in the heavy white dress. Hendrik is on hands and knees trying to crawl after her. I retreat to the dark of my room to wait for the noises to cease.

198. Gun in hand I emerge on to the bare stoep. I raise it and aim at the patch of white shirt. The barrel wavers crazily, there is nowhere to rest it. Anna screams and points at me. They spring into motion, running like hares across the yard towards the vegetable garden. I cannot make the gun follow them fast enough. I am not bad, I am not even dangerous. I close my eyes and pull the trigger. I am stunned and deafened, there is a ringing in my ears. Hendrik and Klein-Anna have vanished behind the row of fig-trees. I put the gun back in its place.

199. Dressed in the finery of dead people they sit on the old bench in the shade of the sering-tree. Hendrik crosses his legs and stretches out his arms along the back rail. Klein-Anna snuggles against his shoulder.

He sees me watching them from the window. He rises and approaches. 'Miss doesn't perhaps have a little tobacco for me?'

200. I lie on my bed with the pillow over my eyes. The door of my room is shut but I know that Hendrik is in the house rummaging through drawers. I would know it if a fly licked its feet in this house.

The door opens. I turn to the wall. He stands over me.

'Look, miss, I found some tobacco.'

For the last time I inhale the sweet odour of pipe-tobacco. Who will ever bring it into my house again?

He sits down heavily beside me on the bed. My nostrils fill with his smell. He lays a hand on my hip and I scream at the blank wall, holding my body rigid and bellowing out my terror from the depths of my lungs. The hand leaves me, the smell vanishes, but the screams go on ringing.

201. Hendrik and Klein-Anna sit on the old bench in the shade of the sering-tree. Hendrik crosses his legs and puffs on his pipe. Anna nestles against his shoulder. From the window I watch. They are unscathed.

202. I beckon to Hendrik with the white envelope. 'Take this letter to the post office. Give it to the baas at the post office. He will give you money. If you leave early tomorrow morning, you can be back on Tuesday evening.'

'Yes, miss – the post office.'

'If they ask, say I sent you. Say the baas is sick and can't come. Remember: the baas is sick – don't say anything more.'

'No, miss. The baas is sick.'

'Yes. And tell Anna that if she feels anxious she is welcome to sleep in the kitchen tomorrow night.'

'Yes, miss.'

'And put the letter in a safe place, otherwise you won't get anything.'

'No, miss, I'll keep it safe.'

203. Anna begins to make up her bed. I do not leave the kitchen, but sit against the table watching her. Her movements have grown clumsy. She is out of her depth now that her husband is absent.

'Do you like sleeping in the kitchen, Anna?'

'Yes, miss.' She averts her face, she whispers, she does not know what to do with her hands.

'Don't you want to sleep in a proper bed?'

She is bewildered.

'Don't you want to sleep in the bed in the guest-room?'

'No, miss.'

'What! Do you prefer to sleep here on the floor?'

'Yes, miss, on the floor.'

She endures a long silence. I fill the kettle.

'Get into bed. I am just going to make a cup of tea.'

She covers herself and turns away from the light.

'Tell me, don't you undress, Anna? Don't you undress when you go to sleep? Do you keep your kerchief on when you sleep?'

She pushes the kerchief off.

'Tell me, do you sleep with your clothes on when your husband is with you? That I can't believe.' I pull a chair over to the bedside. 'Do you have a nice time with your husband, Anna? Come on, you don't have to be shy, no one will hear us. Come, tell me, do you have a nice time? Is it nice to be married?' She snuffles miserably, trapped in the dark house with the witchwoman. This is not going to be a dialogue, thank God, I can stretch my wings and fly where I will. 'I too would like a man, but it has not been possible, I have never pleased anyone enough, I have never been pretty.' I crane over her from the stiff kitchen chair and hector; she hears only waves of rage crashing in my voice, and sobs drearily. 'But that is not the worst. Energy is eternal delight, I could have been a quite different person, I could have burned my way out of this prison, my tongue is forked with fire, do you understand; but it has all been turned uselessly inward, what sounds to you like rage is only the crackling of the fire within, I have never been really cross with you, I only wanted to talk, I have never learned to talk with another person. It has always been that the word has come down to me and I have passed it on. I have never known words of true exchange, Anna. The words I give you you cannot give back. They are words without value. Do you understand? No value. What was it like with my father when the two of you spoke? Were you at last simply man and woman? Come, tell me, I want to know. Did he give you good words? Don't cry, child, I told you I am not cross.' I lie down beside her and cradle her head on my arm. She puts out a long tongue and licks the snot from her upper lip. 'Come, stop all this crying. You must believe me, I am not in the least cross about what you and the baas did together. It is good that he found a little happiness with you, he had a terribly lonely life. And I am sure it was nice for both of you, wasn't it? I could never make him happy, I was never more than the dull dutiful daughter, I only bored him.

'Tell me, Anna, if the two of you were together, if he had lived, do you think that it would have been possible that you and I would have been friends? What do you think? I think we would have. I think we would have been something like sisters or cousins.

'Listen, don't move, I am going to blow out the light, then I'll come and lie next to you till you fall asleep.'

I lie trembling beside her in the dark.

'Tell me, Anna, what do you call me? What is my name?' I breathe as softly as I can. 'What do you call me in your thoughts?'

'Miss?'

'Yes; but to you am I only the miss? Have I no name of my own?'

'Miss Magda?'

'Yes; or just plain Magda. After all, Magda is the name I was baptized with, not Miss Magda. Wouldn't it sound strange if the minister baptized the children like that – Miss Magda, Baas Johannes, and so forth?'

I hear a little pop of saliva as she smiles. I am gaining ground.

'Or Klein-Anna, Little Anna, instead of Anna. We are all little to begin with, aren't we. I was once also Little Magda. But now I am just Magda, and you are just Anna. Can you say Magda? Come, say Magda for me.'

'No, miss, I can't.'

'Magda. It's easy. Never mind, tomorrow night we'll try again, then we'll see whether you can say Magda. Now we must sleep. I'll lie with you for a while, then I'll go to my own bed. Goodnight, Anna.'

'Goodnight, miss.'

I find her head and press my lips against her forehead. For a moment she struggles, then stiffens and endures me. We lie together, at odds, I waiting for her to fall asleep, she waiting for me to go.

I grope my way out of the kitchen to my own bed. I am doing my best in this unfamiliar world of touch.

204. I wait for Hendrik. The day passes uneasily. Then far across the veld I see what can only be he toiling towards the house, first a tiny white dustcloud on the horizon, then a dark speck moving against the stillness of other dark specks, then visibly a man on a bicycle pumping himself toward me through the heat of the afternoon. I fold my hands.

Now he has dismounted and is pushing his bicycle through the soft sand where the road crosses the river. He seems to be bringing a parcel. But as he gets nearer the parcel becomes more and more clearly his jacket tied on to the back of the bicycle.

He rests the bicycle against the bottom step and marches up to me. He holds out a letter folded in four.

'Good afternoon, Hendrik, I'm sure you're exhausted. I put some food aside for you.'

'Yes, miss.'

He is waiting for me to read. I unfold the letter. It is nothing but a printed form headed ONTTREKKINGS–WITH-DRAWALS. In the margin there is a pencilled cross against the line *Handtekening van beléer – Signature of depositor.*

'Wouldn't they give you anything?'

'No, miss. Miss said I would get my money. Where is my money now?' He stands so close over me that I am trapped in my chair.

'I am sorry, Hendrik, I am truly sorry. But I'll think of something, don't worry. I'll go to the station myself tomorrow and fix it up. We'll have to catch the donkeys before sunset. I have no idea where they are grazing.' Words, words: I am talking simply to hold back the wall of his anger that towers over me.

I push my chair back and rise unsteadily. He does not retreat an inch. As I turn I brush against the patched shirt, the gleaming skin, the smell of sun and sweat. He follows me in.

205. I point to the covered dish on the table. 'Why don't you eat here in the kitchen?'

He lifts the cover and looks at the cold sausage and cold potatoes.

'I will make tea. You must be thirsty.'

He skims the dish across the table. It shatters on the tiles, the food spilling lumpily everywhere.

'You – !' I scream. He watches to see what I will do. 'In God's name what is wrong? Why can't you tell me straight out why you are so cross? Pick up that food, clean up, I'm not having you make a mess in my house!'

He leans on the table breathing heavily. A fine chest, strong lungs. A man.

'Miss lied!' I hear the words reverberate in the space between us. My heart sinks, I do not want to be shouted at, it only leaves me helpless. 'Miss said the post office would give me money! Two days I rode – two days! And where is my money? How must I live? The storeroom is empty. Where must we get food? From heaven? While the baas was here we got our food every week, our money every month; but where is the baas lying now?'

Does he not see that this achieves nothing? What can I do? I have no money to give him. 'You may as well leave,' I mumble, but he does not hear me, he is ranting, throwing heavy black words which I no longer bother to catch.

I turn to go. He springs at me and grabs my arm. 'Let go!' I shout. He grips me tightly and pulls me back into the kitchen. 'No, wait a bit!' he hisses in my ear. I pick up the first thing I see, a fork, and lunge at him. The tines scrape his shoulder, probably not even piercing the skin; but he exclaims in surprise

113

and hurls me to the floor. I stumble up into a deluge of blows. I have no breath left, everything has been gasped out, I cover my head and fall slowly and awkwardly back to the floor. 'Yes! . . . Yes! . . . Yes! . . .' says Hendrik, beating me, I raise myself on hands and knees and begin to crawl to the door. He kicks me in the buttocks, heavily, twice, a man's kicks, catching bone. I flinch and weep with shame.

'Please, please!' I roll over on my back and lift my knees. This is how a bitch must look; but as for what happens next, I do not even know how it is done. He goes on kicking at my thighs.

206. Hendrik still rants behind me, throwing his heavy black words, but I cannot listen to more of this grudge from a man ridden by a sense of being wronged. I turn and walk out. At my second step he is upon me, catching my arm and yanking me round. I struggle against him. I pick up the first thing I see, a fork, and lunge with it, scraping his shoulder. The skin is not even pierced, but he sucks in his breath with surprise and hurls me against the wall, his whole weight upon me. The fork falls. His pelvis grinds hard into me. 'No!' I say. 'Yes!' he grunts an inch from my ear, 'Yes! . . . Yes! . . .' I weep, the situation is shameful, I do not see how to get out of it, something is going limp inside me, something is dying. He bends and fumbles for the bottom of my dress. I scuffle, but he finds it and his fingers come up between my legs. I grip as tightly as I can to keep them still. 'No, please not, please, not that, only not that, I beg you, Hendrik, I will give you anything, only please not that!' I am light-headed with panting, I push and push at his face without effect. He slides down my body, dragging at the elastic of my pants, scratching me. 'No! . . . No! . . . No! . . .' I am faint with fright, there is no pleasure in this. 'Ah Hendrik, please let me go, I don't even know how!' I am falling, perhaps even fainting, held up only by his arms around my thighs. Then I am lying on the floor smelling the beeswax, the dust. I am

nauseous with fear, my limbs have turned to water. If this is my fate it sickens me.

Things are happening to me, things are being done to me, I feel them far away, terrible incisions, dull surgery. Sounds come clearly: suckings, breathings, lappings. 'Not here, not on the floor, please, please!' His ear is at my lips, I need only whisper to be heard. He rocks me back and forth, back and forth on the floorboards, my skull giving a little bump on the skirting every time. Smells come clearly too, hair, ash. 'You are hurting me . . . please . . . please stop . . .' Is this finally how people do it? He heaves on and on, he groans against my ear, tears run down the back of my throat. Let it stop, let it stop! He begins to pant. He shudders lengthily and lies still on me. Then he draws himself out and away. Now I know for sure he was inside me, now that he is out and all the ache and clamminess sets in. I press my fingers into my groin while beside me he fastens his trousers. It is beginning to seep out of me, this acrid flow that must be his seed, down my thighs, on to my clothes, on to the floor. How can I ever wash it all out? I sob and sob in despair.

207. He throws me against the wall, pinning my wrists, his whole weight upon me. The fork falls to the floor, his pelvis grinds hard into me. 'No!' I say. 'Yes!' he says, 'Yes! . . . Yes! . . .' 'Why do you hate me so?' I sob. I turn my face from him, I cannot help it. 'You only want to hurt me all the time. What have I done to you? It is not my fault that everything is going so badly, it is your wife's fault, it is her fault and my father's. And it's also your fault! You people don't know where to stop! Stop it! Don't do that, you're hurting me! Please stop it! Why are you hurting me? Why do you hurt me so much? Please! Please not like this on the floor! Let me go, Hendrik!'

208. He closes the bedroom door and stands against it. 'Take off your clothes!' says this stranger. He forces me to undress. My fingers are numb. I am shivering. I whisper to myself without cease, but he is lost in himself, he does not hear me.

'You do nothing but shout at me, you never talk to me, you hate me . . .' I turn my back on him and find my way gracelessly out of my dress and petticoat. This is my fate, this is a woman's fate. I cannot do more than I have done. I lie down on the bed with my back to him, hugging and hiding my mean little breasts. I have forgotten to take my shoes off! It is too late now, things will follow on from a beginning to an end. I must simply endure until finally I am left alone and can begin to rediscover who I am, putting together, in the time of which there is blessedly so much here, the pieces that this unusual afternoon in my life is disarranging.

209. Pulling off my pants he rips them on the shoebuttons: more womanwork for me. 'Open up,' he says, those are his first words to me; but I am cold, I shake my head and clench myself, I clench everything together, I have nothing to give him, I am beyond being persuaded, even the tears can find no way out from behind these knotted eyelids, he will have to break me open, I am as hard as shell, I cannot help him. He parts my knees by force and I clamp them to again, time after time after time.

He lifts my legs in the air. I stiffen and cry out with shame. 'Don't be afraid,' he says. Are those his words? His tongue is thick. Then suddenly his head pushes in between my thighs. I press against his woolly hair, I squirm, but he burrows in. 'Aah . . .' I cry, there is no end to the humiliation. I am soggy, it is revolting, it must be with his spit, he must have spat on me while he was there. I sob and sob.

He crouches between my legs, holding them apart and pushing. 'It won't hurt,' he says.

He has forced his way into me. I toss from side to side and weep, but he is relentless, he bares my breasts too and presses down on me; he pants in my ear, rocking further and further in, when will it stop? 'Everyone likes it,' he says harshly. Are those his words? What does he mean? And then: 'Hold tight!' What? The bed creaks at every joint, it is a single bed, a divan, it was not made for this. He sucks the breath out of my lungs, he moans and hisses in my ear, his teeth grind like stones. 'Everyone likes it'? 'Everyone likes it'? Can people be so affected? But by what? Shudders run through him from head to foot, I feel them distinctly, more distinctly than anything else yet, this must be the climax of the act, this I know, this I have seen in animals, it is the same everywhere, it signals the end.

210. He lies beside me on his back, snoring, asleep. My hand covers his man's part, held there by his hand; but my nerves are dull, I am without curiosity, I feel only a dampness and softness. Without disturbing him I pull the green counterpane over myself. Am I now a woman? Has this made me into a woman? So many tiny events, acts, movements one after another, muscles pulling bones this way and that, and their upshot is that I can say, I am finally a woman, or, Am I finally a woman? Fingers grip the spine of a fork, the tines flash out, plunging through the patched shirt, ploughing through the skin. Blood flows. Two arms grapple, the fork falls. A body lies on top of a body pushing and pushing, trying to find a way in, motion everywhere. But what does this body want inside me? What is this man trying to find in me? Will he try again when he wakes up? What deeper invasion and possession does he plot in his sleep? That one day all his bony frame shall lie packed inside me, his skull inside my skull, his limbs along my limbs, the rest of him crammed into my belly? What will he leave me of myself?

211. The last of the afternoon is wheeling past while I lie beside this man seeping tears and blood. If I were to get up now and walk, for I can still walk, I can still talk, if I were to walk out on to the stoep, my hair tangled, my buttocks sagging, my thighs smeared in filth, if I were to come out into the light, I, the black flower that grows in the corner, dazzled, dizzy, I am sure that in spite of all it would be an afternoon like any other, the cicadas would not pause in their grating, the heat-

waves would still thrill on the horizon, the sun would still lie ponderous and indifferent on my skin. I have been through everything now and no angel has descended with flaming sword to forbid it. There are, it seems, no angels in this part of the sky, no God in this part of the world. It belongs only to the sun. I do not think it was ever intended that people should live here. This is a land made for insects who eat sand and lay eggs in each other's corpses and have no voices with which to scream when they die. It would cost me nothing to go to the kitchen and fetch a knife and cut off the part of this man with which he has been offending me. Where will it all end? What is there left for me now? When will I be able to say, It is enough? I long for the end. I long to be folded in someone's arms, to be soothed and fondled and told I may stop ticking. I want a cave, a hole to snuggle in, I want to block my ears against this chatter that streams endlessly from and into me, I want a home somewhere else, if it has to be in this body then on different terms in this body, if there is no other body, though there is one I would far prefer, I cannot stop these words unless I cut my throat, I would like to climb into Klein-Anna's body, I would like to climb down her throat while she sleeps and spread myself gently inside her, my hands in her hands, my feet in her feet, my skull in the benign quiet of her skull where images of soap and flour and milk revolve, the holes of my body sliding into place over the holes of hers, there to wait mindlessly for whatever enters them, the song of birds, the smell of dung, the parts of a man, not angry now but gentle, rocking in my bloodwarmth, laving me with soapy seed, sleeping in my cave. I too am falling asleep as my fingers, covered by his sleeping fingers, begin to learn to caress this soft thing for which I will probably, as long as I am able, try not to learn the name.

212. He pushes my hand away and sits up.

'You have been sleeping.' They are my words, soft, from me. How strange. They just come. 'Please don't be cross any more. I won't say anything.' I turn on my side and look full at him.

He rubs his face in his cupped hands, climbs over me, and finds his trousers. I lean on an elbow watching the brisk movements with which men dress.

He leaves the room, and a moment later I hear the tyres of his bicycle crunch on the gravel, softer and softer as he rides off.

213. I knock at the open door of the cottage. I am washed, my face feels clean and kind. Anna comes up behind me carrying an armful of firewood.

'Evening, Anna, is Hendrik at home?'

'Yes, miss. Hendrik! The miss is here!'

So she knows nothing. I smile at her and she flinches. It will take time.

Hendrik stands in the doorway, keeping to the shadow.

'Hendrik, will you and Anna come and sleep in the house from now on, I get too nervous when I am alone. I'll give you proper beds, you won't have to sleep on the floor again. In fact, there is no reason why you shouldn't sleep in the guestroom. Bring along everything you will need, then you won't have to run back and forth.'

They exchange looks while I stand waiting.

'Yes, we'll come,' says Hendrik.

214. We sit all three around the kitchen table eating by candlelight the soup that Anna and I have made. Unsure of their footing here, unsure of my customs, they eat awkwardly. Anna casts her eyes down; Hendrik answers my questions about the farm in his old curt way.

215. I wash the dishes and Anna dries. We work deftly together. It is the moments when her hands have no work that she fears. I am resolved to ask fewer questions and to chatter more, so that she will grow accustomed to the declarative mode. At the moments when our bodies brush I am careful not to pull back.

Hendrik has vanished into the night. What do men do when they walk about in the dark?

216. We make up two beds in the guestroom, decently, with sheets and blankets. Then we push the beds together. I see to it that there is a chamberpot. I fill the waterjug. I am failing in no observance, nor are my intentions impure. In the heart of nowhere, in this dead place, I am making a start; or, if not that, making a gesture.

217. In the small hours of the night Hendrik creeps into my bed and takes me. It hurts, I am still raw, but I try to relax, to understand the sensation, though as yet it has no form. I do not see what it is in me that causes his excitement; or if I do recognize the cause, I hope that in time it will change for the better. I would like to sleep in his arms, to see whether it is possible to sleep in someone else's arms, but that is not what he wants. I do not yet like the smell of his seed. Does a woman grow used to it, I wonder. Anna must on no account make up this bed in the morning. I must rub salt into the bloody sheets and lock them away, or else quietly burn them.

Hendrik rises and dresses in the dark. I have had no sleep, it is nearly morning, I am dizzy with exhaustion.

'Am I doing it right, Hendrik?' I lean out from the bed and catch his hand. I can hear from my voice, and he must hear it too, that I am changing. 'I don't know anything about this, Hendrik – do you understand? All I want to know is whether I am doing it right. Please give me just that little help.'

He loosens my fingers, not unkindly, and departs. I lie naked, pondering, making the most of the time that is mine before first light, preparing myself too for the night to come.

218. 'Are you happy, Hendrik? Do I make you feel happy?' I run my fingers over his face, this is something he allows me. His mouth is not smiling, but a smiling mouth is not the sole sign of happiness. 'Do you like what we do? Hendrik, I know

nothing. I don't know whether you like what we do. Do you understand what I am telling you?'

I would like a chance to look at him, I would like to see whether he regards me with the old watchfulness. His face is growing more obscure to me every day.

I lean over him, stroking him with swings of my hair, it is something he seems to like, it is something he allows me. 'Hendrik, why won't you let me light a candle? Just once? You come in the night like a ghost – how am I to know it is really you?'

'Who else would it be?'

'No one . . . I just want to see how you look. May I?'

'No, don't!'

219. Some nights he does not come. I lie naked, waiting, dozing into shallow sleep, snapping awake, groaning at the first birdsong, the first aura of dawn. This too happens to women, they lie waiting for men who do not come, I have read of it, let it not be said that I do not undergo everything, from the first letter to the last.

I am growing limp with lack of sleep. I fall asleep without warning in the afternoons, slumped in a chair anywhere, and wake hot and confused, the last thin echo of a snore in my ears. Do the two of them see me like this? Do they point at me and smile and tiptoe about their business? I grind my teeth with shame.

220. I am eating badly, growing even scrawnier, if that is possible. I suffer from rashes about the neck. I have no beauty to lure him on with. Perhaps that is why he will not allow a candle, perhaps he thinks he would be put off by the sight of me. I do not know what pleases him, whether he wants me to move or lie still when he takes me. I stroke his skin but feel no response from it. He stays with me more and more briefly, sometimes for only the minute it takes him to release himself inside me. He does not take off his shirt. I am too dry for this

kind of activity. I have begun with it too late in life, streams that should be running dried up long ago. I try to moisten myself when I hear him at the door, but it does not always work. I cannot honestly see why he leaves his wife's bed for mine. Sometimes the fishy smell of her comes to my nostrils when he undresses. I am sure they make love every night.

221. He turns me on my face and does it to me from behind like an animal. Everything dies in me when I have to raise my ugly rear to him. I am humiliated; sometimes I think it is my humiliation he wants.

222. 'Stay just a moment longer, Hendrik. Can't we talk? We get so little chance to talk to each other.'

'Ssh, not so loud, she will hear us!'

'She is a child, she is fast asleep! Do you mind if she finds out?'

'No. What can she do? What can brown people do?'

'Please, don't be so bitter! What have I done to make you so bitter?'

'Nothing, miss.'

He is scrambling out of the bed, his body as unyielding as iron.

'Hendrik, don't go! I am tired, tired to the marrow of my bones. Can't you understand? All I want is a little peace between us. It isn't much to ask for.'

'No, miss.' And he is gone.

223. There are the days to fill too, days of atomic aimlessness. We three cannot find our true paths in this house. I cannot say whether Hendrik and Anna are guests or invaders or prisoners. I can no longer shut myself off in my room as I used to do. I cannot leave Anna to fend for herself in the house. I watch her eyes, waiting for her to reveal that she knows what happens in the nights; but she will not look at me. We still work together in the kitchen. Beyond that, what can I expect of her? Must

she be the one who keeps the house shining or must I, while she watches? Must we kneel and polish together, servitors of a domestic ideal? She wants to go back to her own home, I know, back to her own lax ways and comfortable smells. It is Hendrik who is keeping her here. She must want to be alone with Hendrik. But Hendrik wants both her and me as I want both her and Hendrik. I do not know how to resolve the problem. I know nothing save that asymmetry makes people unhappy.

224. Anna is oppressed by my watching eyes. She is oppressed by my invitations to relax, to sit by my side on the old bench in the shade of the sering-tree. She is oppressed particularly by my talk. I no longer ask her questions, I know better than that, I simply speak to her; but I have no skill in speech, I know no anecdotes, no gossip, I have lived all my life alone, I have no experience to draw on, my speech is sometimes mere babble, sometimes I see myself as a boring child babbling to her, learning a human tongue, certainly, in the course of babbling, but slowly, too slowly, and at too great a cost. As for her words, they come to me dull with reluctance.

225. I announce that the day has come to make green fig preserve. I am gay, it is a favourite day of mine, but I cannot rouse Anna from her morose fit. We move down the rows of trees. Pick only the smallest figs, I tell her, pick nothing that has so much as begun to ripen. For every five that fall into my bucket one falls into hers. We spread the figs on the kitchen table. Cut a little cross like this, I tell her, so that the sugar can work its way in to the core. My fingers are nimble, hers are thick, she works slowly, she is no help. She drops her hands into her lap and sighs. I watch from across the table, across the bowls of figs. She will not meet my eyes.

'Is there something upsetting you, child?' I ask. 'Come on, tell me, perhaps I can help.'

She shakes her head miserably, stupidly. She picks up a fig and scrapes at it.

'Are you lonely, Anna? Are you longing to see your family?'

She shakes her head slowly.

This is how I spend my days. There has been no transfiguration. What I long for, whatever it is, does not come.

226. I stand behind Anna. I put my hands on her shoulders, I slip my fingers under the neck of her dress and caress the clear young bones, the clavicle, the scapula, names telling nothing of their beauty. She sinks her head.

'Sometimes I too feel full of sorrow. I am sure it is the landscape that makes us feel like that.' My fingers touch her throat, her jaw, her temples. 'Never mind. Soon it will all come right.'

What does one do with desire? My eye falls idly on objects, odd stones, pretty flowers, strange insects: I pick them up, bear them home, store them away. A man comes to Anna and comes to me: we embrace him, we hold him inside us, we are his, he is ours. I am heir to a space of natal earth which my ancestors found good and fenced about. To the spur of desire we have only one response: to capture, to enclose, to hold. But how real is our possession? The flowers turn to dust, Hendrik uncouples and leaves, the land knows nothing of fences, the stones will be here when I have crumbled away, the very food I devour passes through me. I am not one of the heroes of desire, what I want is not infinite or unattainable, all I ask myself, faintly, dubiously, querulously, is whether there is not something to do with desire other than striving to possess the desired in a project which must be vain, since its end can only be the annihilation of the desired. And how much keener does my question become when woman desires woman, two holes, two emptinesses. For if that is what I am then that is what she is too, anatomy is destiny: an emptiness, or a shell, a film over an emptiness longing to be filled in a world in which nothing fills. I speak to her: 'Do you know what I feel like, Anna? Like a great emptiness, an emptiness filled with a great absence, an absence which is a desire to be filled, to be fulfilled. Yet at the same time I know that nothing will fill me, because it is the first condition of life forever to desire, otherwise life would cease. It is a principle of life forever to be unfulfilled. Fulfilment does not fulfil. Only stones desire nothing. And who knows, perhaps in stones there are also holes we have never discovered.'

I lean over her, I caress her arms, I hold her limp hands in mine. That is what she gets from me, colonial philosophy, words with no history behind them, homespun, when she wants stories. I can imagine a woman who would make this child happy, filling her with tales from a past that really happened, how grandfather ran away from the bees and lost his hat and never found it again, why the moon waxes and wanes, how the hare tricked the jackal. But these words of mine come from nowhere and go nowhere, they have no past or future, they whistle across the flats in a desolate eternal present, feeding no one.

227. We have had visitors.

Anna was cutting my hair. I sat on a stool outside the kitchen in the cool of the morning. From across the lands the breeze brought the muffled subterranean clang of the pump, another sound in a world full of familiar evocative sounds. I can conceive of myself blind and happy in a world like this, raising my face to the sun and basking, tuning my ears to the distance. Anna's scissors slide cool across the nape of my neck, obedient to my murmurs.

Then all at once there is tumult in the empty doorway, brown on grey on black, the space discomposing and recomposing itself before my eyes, and Hendrik has come and gone, his trouserlegs whipping against each other, his soles crunching the gravel; and Anna at once behind him running too, bent, urgent, the comb and scissors scattering, from stillness into motion without transition as if all her life with me has only been an instant frozen, abstracted, stolen from a life of running. Before I can stand up they are gone behind the wall of the shearing-pens, behind the wagonhouse, down the slope into the riverbed.

With the tablecloth over my shoulders and my halfcut hair in my fist I emerge from the house to face two strangers, two horsemen. Unkempt, surprised, is is I who ought to be at a disadvantage; but I know better, they are on my land, they have disturbed me, it is they who have to make their apologies and state their business.

'No,' I tell them curtly, 'he left early this morning . . . No, I don't know where . . . The boy went with him . . . Probably late. He always comes home late.'

They are father and son, neighbours. When did I last see a neighbour? Have I ever seen one? They do not say why they have come. They come on men's business. Fences are down, a dog-pack is at large, there is an epidemic among the sheep, the locusts are swarming, the shearers have not arrived, they will not tell me what. These are real calamities, how will I ever deal with them by myself? If I make Hendrik my foreman will he be able to run the farm while I stand severely behind him pretending he is my puppet? Would it not be better to span barbed wire around the farm, lock the gates, kill off the sheep, and give up the fiction of farming? How can I convince hardened men like these that I am of their stuff when patently I am not? They have ridden far on a futile errand, they are waiting for an invitation to dismount and take refreshment; but I continue to stand silent and forbidding before them till, exchanging glances, they tip their hats and turn their horses.

These are trying times. There are going to be more visits, harder questions to answer, before the visits and the questions stop. There will be much temptation to grovel and weep. How idyllic the old days seem; and how alluring, in a different way, a future in a garden behind barbed wire! Two stories to comfort myself with: for the truth is, I fear, that there is no past or future, that the medium I live in is an eternal present in which, whether heaving under the weight of that hard man or feeling the ice of the scissors-blade at my ear or washing the dead or dressing meat, I am the reluctant polestar about which all this phenomenal universe spins. I am pressed but not possessed, I am pierced but my core is not touched. At heart I am still the fierce mantis virgin of yore. Hendrik may take me, but it is I holding him holding I.

228. 'They will come again! You can't fool around with those people! They will be expecting the old baas to come, and if he does not they will know there is something wrong!'

He strides in and out of the pool of lamplight. He has returned by night bringing the tempest with him. Now I can truly see how far we have progressed in familiarity. He has learned to leave his hat on in my presence. He has learned to storm up and down while he talks, striking his fist into his palm. His gestures express anger, but also the confidence of a man free to show his anger. It is interesting. What passion he has shown for me has been a passion of rage. That is why my body has locked itself against him. Unloved, it has been unloving. But has it been hated? What is it that he has been trying to do all this time? There is something he has been trying to force from my body, I know, but I have been too obstinate, too awkward, too lumpish, too stale, too tired, too frightened by the flow of his angry corrosive seed; I have merely gritted my teeth and clung on when he wanted something else, to touch my heart perhaps, to touch my heart and convulse me. How deep, I wonder, can one person go into another? What a pity that he cannot show me. He has the means but not the words, I the words but not the means; for there is nowhere, I fear, where my words will not reach.

'I am telling you, one of these days they will be back, sooner than you think, along with other people, all the other farmers! Then they will see that you are living with the servants in the big house. Then *we* will be the ones to suffer not you she and I!'

'And they will find out about the old baas too, you can be sure of that! That old Anna has been spreading stories for a long time, everyone knows that the old baas was messing around with my wife. So when they say I shot him, who will believe me, who will believe a brown man? They will hang me! Me! No – I'm leaving, I'm leaving tomorrow, I'm getting out of this part of the world, by tomorrow night I want to be far away, I want to be at the Cape!'

'Hendrik, can we speak reasonably for a moment? Will you please sit down, I get confused when you storm around like that. Tell me first, where were you all day and where is Anna?'

'Anna is at home. We are not sleeping here any more.'

'Are you also not sleeping here? Do I have to sleep alone in this house?'

'We are not sleeping here.'

'Do you know, Hendrik, you hurt me. Do you know, you have the power to hurt me, and you do it every time. Do you really think I would turn you over to the police? Do you think I am too spineless to acknowledge my guilt? If so, you don't know me, Hendrik. You are so bitter that you are completely blinded. I am not simply one of the whites, I am I! I am I, not a people. Why have I to pay for other people's sins? You know how I live here on the farm, totally outside human society, almost outside humanity! Look at me! You know who I am, I don't have to tell you! You know what they call me, the witch of Agterplaas! Why should I side with them against you? I am telling you the truth! What *more* do I have to do before you will believe I am telling the truth! Can't you see that you and Anna are the only people in the world I am attached to? What more do you want? Must I weep? Must I kneel? Are you waiting for the white woman to kneel to you? Are you waiting for me to become your white slave? *Tell me! Speak!* Why do you never *say* anything? Why is it that you take me every night if you hate me? Why won't you even tell me if I do it right? How am I to know? How am I to learn? Who must I ask? Must I ask Anna? Must I really go and ask your own wife how to be a woman? How can I humiliate myself any further? Must the white woman lick your backside before you will give her a single smile? Do you know that you have never kissed me, never, never, never? Don't you people ever kiss? Don't you ever kiss your wife? What is it that makes her so different from me? Does a woman have to hurt you before you can love her? Is that your secret, Hendrik?'

Where was it in this torrent of pleas and accusations that he walked out? Did he stay to the end? Is he lost to me forever? Would it be possible, if I smiled more, if I could make my body thaw, to rediscover the patient young man I once knew who made his own shoes, who turned the handle of the coffee-grinder while I poured the beans, who tipped his hat and flashed his teeth and loped off to his next task with that relaxed, tireless stride? In knowing him better I seem to have lost all that I liked best in him. What is the lesson I should learn, if it is not too late for all lessons, if I am ever to know a man again? Is it the lesson my father learned when he could not raise a hand to wave the flies from his face: Beware of intimacy with the servants? Is it that Hendrik and I are, in our different ways, ruined for love? Or is it simply that the story took a wrong turn somewhere, that if I had found a more gradual path to a gentler form of intimacy we might all have learned to be happy together? Or is this desert of fire and ice a purgatory we must pass through on the way to a land of milk and honey? And what of Anna? Will she come too? Will she and I one day be sisters and sleep in the same bed? Or will she, when she finds herself, scratch my eyes out?

229. There must be other ways of filling empty days than by dusting and sweeping and polishing. I move through the cycle of rooms like a mouse in a treadmill. Is there no way of cleaning a room definitively? Perhaps if I begin again in the loft, plugging the gaps between roof and walls, pinning paper over the floor, perhaps if then I seal and caulk the doors and windows, I can halt the sift of dust and leave the house till the coming of spring, if spring ever comes again, if anyone is here in springtime to unlock. Perhaps I can leave one room open, my own preferably, for old times' sake, and pile in it the last of the candles, the last

of the food, hatchet, hammer, nails, the last of the paper and ink. Or perhaps it would be better to close the shutters, lock the last door, and move my effects into the dim little storehouse where the builders of the great house lived when long ago they plotted the feudal dynasty to come. There, among the mice and cockroaches, I might surely find a way of winding down my history.

230. One by one the doors of the great house click shut behind me. Shuffling furniture, capturing dirt, turning wood to ash I have found occupation for a lifetime. Slaves lose everything in their chains, I recognize, even joy in escaping from them. The host is dying, the parasite scuttles anxiously about the cooling entrails wondering whose tissues it will live off next.

I was not, after all, made to live alone. If I had been set down by fate in the middle of the veld in the middle of nowhere, buried to my waist and commanded to live a life, I could not have done it. I am not a philosopher. Women are not philosophers, and I am a woman. A woman cannot make something out of nothing. However sterile my occupation with dust and cobwebs and food and soiled linen may have seemed, it was necessary to fill me out, to give me life. Alone in the veld I would pine away. Out of the movements of the heavenly bodies and the tiny signals of insects debating whether or not I might yet be eaten I could not possibly fill day after day and night after night. I would need at the very least, besides eyes and ears, two hands and the use of them, and a store of pebbles to build patterns with: and how long can one go on building patterns before one longs for extinction? I am not a principle, a rule of discourse, a machine planted by a being from another planet on this desolate earth beneath the Southern Cross to generate sentiments day after day, night after night, keeping count of them as I go, until I run dry. I need more than merely pebbles to permute, rooms to clean, furniture to push around: I need people to talk to, brothers and sisters or fathers and mothers, I need a history and a culture, I need hopes and aspirations, I need a moral sense and a teleology before I will be happy, not to mention food and drink. What will become of me now that I am alone? For I am alone again, alone in the historical present: Hendrik is gone, Anna is gone with him, they fled in the night without a word, taking nothing that could not be strapped on a bicycle. What is going to happen now? I am full of foreboding. I huddle in the storeroom, the chill of the stone floor seeps into my bones, the cockroaches stand around me waving their curious antennae, and I fear the very worst.

231. Winter is coming. A cold wind whistles across the flats beneath an iron sky. The potatoes have gone to seed, the fruit has rotted on the ground. The dog has departed, following Hendrik. The pumps spin monotonously day and night, the dams flow over. The farm is going to ruin. I do not know what will happen to the sheep. I have opened every gate on the farm, they have spread into every camp. One morning before dawn a hundred grey shapes passed between house and store-room, a muted thudding and jostling, in search of new pasture. I find that they mean nothing to me. I cannot catch them, I have not the stomach to slaughter them. If I had bullets I would shoot them for their own good (I weigh the gun in my hand, my arm is steady) and leave them to moulder. Their fleece is long and filthy; infested with ticks and blowfly, they cannot survive another summer.

232. I live on pumpkin and mealie-porridge. I have put away nothing for the hard days ahead. God will provide for his own; and if I am not one of his own, it were as well I should perish. I trudge about my trivial businesses whipped by the wind. Particle by particle the skin is flayed from my face; I have no will to regenerate it. Atoms of skin, atoms of mortar, atoms of rust fly off into oblivion. If one is very patient, if one lives long enough, one can hope to see the day when the last wall falls

to dust, the lizard suns itself on the hearth, the thornbush sprouts in the graveyard.

233. I have had visitors, more visitors than I can name. I did not know, in my aboriginal innocence, that there were so many people in the world. Every inch of the farm has been searched for my father, who rode out one ill-fated day and never came back.

The name cannot be crossed off the list, they explain to me, until the remains are discovered. That is the principle. I nod. How fortunate one must be to have simple, credible principles to live by. Perhaps it is not too late to leave the wilds and find a home in civilization.

234. The horse. The horse stood in the stable for weeks after the disappearance of my father. Then I tired of feeding the horse and turned it loose. Now there is no horse. Or perhaps the horse roams the hills looking for its lost master.

235. Ou-Anna and Jakob have visited the farm too. They came in the donkey-cart to fetch their last belongings. Ou-Anna sighed and spoke of my father's virtues. 'He was always a man of his word,' she said. 'What news do you have of Hendrik?' I said. 'Nothing,' she said, 'he has disappeared, he and that wife of his. But they will catch him yet!'

Jakob presses his hat to his chest and bows. His wife guides him to the cart. She whips up the donkeys and they trundle out of my life, wizened, hunched. I watch until they cross the drift, then I close the door.

236. What will become of Hendrik? When they came to search for my father, those bearded men, those boys with the rosy cheeks and the strict little mouths and the marksmen's blue eyes, were they truly searching for the absent master or were they after the truant slave and his mate? And if the latter, must they not have found them by now, and laconically shot

them, and gone home to their suppers? For in this part of the world there is no hiding-place. This part of the world is naked in every direction to the eye of the hunter; he who cannot burrow is lost.

But perhaps they did not shoot them out of hand. Perhaps, having tracked them down, they took them in, tied like beasts, to some far-off place of justice and condemned them to break stone for the rest of their lives to pay for their crimes and the crazed vindictive stories they told. Perhaps, as a woman, as a maiden lady weak in the head, I was told nothing. Perhaps they marched Hendrik and Anna out of the courtroom and looked at each other and nodded, tempering justice with mercy, and sent the bailiff with a roll of wire to wire the gates of this farm shut, and cast me out of their minds. For one may be locked away as well in a large space as in a small. Perhaps, therefore, my story has already had its end, the documents tied up with a ribbon and stored away, and only I do not know, for my own good.

Or perhaps they did indeed bring Hendrik back to the farm, to confront me, and I have forgotten. Perhaps they all came, the magistrate, the clerks, the bailiffs, the curious from miles around, and marched Hendrik up to me chained at wrist and ankle, and said, 'Is this the man?' and waited for my answer. Then we looked upon each other for the last time and I said, 'Yes, it's he,' and he swore villainously and spat on me, and they beat him and dragged him off, and I wept. Perhaps that is the true story, however unflattering to me.

Or perhaps I have been mistaken all the time, perhaps my father is not dead after all, but tonight at dusk will come riding out of the hills on the lost horse, and stamp into the house, growling because his bath is not ready, bursting open the locked doors, sniffing at the strange smells. 'Who was here?' shouts my father. 'Have you had a *hotnot* in the house?' I whimper and begin to run, but he catches me and twists my arm. I gibber with fear, 'Hendrik!' I sob, 'Come and help, the ghosts are back!'

But Hendrik, alas, is gone and I must face my demons alone, a grown woman, a woman of the world, though one would not think so, crouched behind the last bag of mealies. Hendrik, I cannot speak to you, but I wish you well, you and Anna both, I wish you the cunning of the jackal, I wish you better luck than your hunters. And if one night you come tapping at the window I will not be surprised. You can sleep here all day, at night you can walk about in the moonlight saying to yourself whatever it is that men say to themselves on a piece of earth that is their own. I will cook your meals, I will even, if you like, try again to be your second woman, it is surely not beyond me if I put my mind to it, all things must be possible on this island out of space, out of time. You can bring your cubs with you; I will guard them by day and take them out to play by night. Their large eyes will glow, they will see things invisible to other folk; and in the daytime when the eye of heaven glowers and pierces every shadow we can lie together in the cool dark of the earth, you and I and Anna and they.

237. Summers and winters come and go. How they pass so swiftly, how many have passed I cannot say, not having had the foresight long ago to start cutting notches in a pole or scratching marks on a wall or keeping a journal like a good castaway. But time has flowed ceaselessly and I am now truly a mad old bad old woman with a stooped back and a hooked nose and knobbly fingers. Perhaps I am wrong to picture time as a river flowing from infinite to infinite bearing me with it like a cork or a twig; or perhaps, having flowed above ground for a while, time flowed underground for a while, and then re-emerged, for reasons forever closed to me, and now flows again in the light, and I flow with it and can be heard again after all those summers and winters in the bowels of the earth during which the words must have gone on (for where would I be if they stopped?) but gone on without trace, without memory. Or perhaps there is no time, perhaps I am deceived when I think of my medium as time, perhaps there is only space, and I a

dot of light moving erratically from one point in space to another, skipping years in a flash, now a frightened child in the corner of a schoolroom, now an old woman with knobbly fingers, that is also possible, my mind is open, and it would explain some of the tentativeness with which I hold my memories.

238. There has been only one more visitor to the farm. The visitor came walking up the road to the house one afternoon. I watched him from the place on the hillside where I work with the stones. He did not see me. He knocked at the kitchen door. Then, shading his eyes, he tried to peer in through a window. He was a child, a boy of twelve or thirteen, dressed in pants that came down to his knees and a baggy brown shirt. On his head he wore some kind of khaki cap or kepi such as I had never seen before. When no one answered his knock he left the house and went down to the orchard, where the orange trees stood full of fruit. It was there that I crept up on him, an old woman of the wilds. He jumped to his feet, trembling, trying to hide a half-eaten orange behind his back.

'And who is stealing my fruit?' I said, the words dropping heavily from my lips, like stones, how strange to speak real words again to a real listener, however petrified.

The child stared back goggle-eyed – let me recreate the scene – at the crone in the black dress flecked with foodstains and verdigris, with the big teeth pointing in all directions and the mad eyes and the mane of grey hair, knowing in that instant that all the stories were true, that worse was true, that he would never see his mother again but be butchered like a lamb and his sweet flesh be roasted in the oven and his sinews boiled down to glue and his eyeballs seethed in a potion and his clean bones thrown to the dogs. 'No, no!' he panted, his little heart almost stopping, and he fell to his knees. From his pocket he pulled out a letter and raised it trembling in the air. 'It's a letter, old miss, please!'

It was a buff envelope with a cross drawn heavily over it in blue pencil. It was addressed to my father. Therefore we were not forgotten.

I opened the envelope. In it was a printed letter in two languages requesting the payment of taxes for road maintenance, vermin eradication, and other marvels I had never heard of.

'Whose signature is this?' I asked the child. He shook his head, watching me, unwilling to come nearer. 'Who sent the letter?'

'Post office, old miss.'

'Yes, but who?'

'Don't know, old miss. Old miss must sign. For the letter.' He held out a little notebook and a stub of pencil.

Holding the book against my thigh I wrote 'I HAVE NO MONEY,' in block letters because of the pain in my fingers.

The child took his book and pencil back from me and put them in his pocket.

'Sit,' I said, and he sat on his heels. 'How old are you?'

'Twelve, old miss.'

'And what is your name?'

'Piet, old miss.'

'Well, Piet, tell me, have you ever done this?' I made a circle of the thumb and first finger of my left hand and plunged the first finger of my right hand back and forth through it.

Piet shook his head slowly, looking straight into my mad old eyes, judging the moment to leap.

I took a step closer and put a hand on his shoulder. 'Would you like to learn, Piet?'

There was a scuffle of dust and he was gone, racing through the orange trees, up the bank, and off up the road with his cap clutched in his hand.

That was the one visit.

239. I also hear voices. It is my commerce with the voices that has kept me from becoming a beast. For I am sure that if the voices did not speak to me I would long ago have given up this articulated chip-chop and begun to howl or bellow or

squawk. The sailor on the desert island speaks to his pets: 'Pretty Polly!' he says to his parrot, 'Fetch!' he says to his dog. But all the time he feels his lips harden, his tongue thicken, his larynx coarsen. 'Woof!' says the dog, 'Squawk!' says the parrot. And soon the sailor is bounding on all fours, clubbing the indigenous goats with thighbones, eating their flesh raw. It is not speech that makes man man but the speech of others.

240. The voices speak to me out of machines that fly in the sky. They speak to me in Spanish.

241. I know no Spanish whatsoever. However, it is characteristic of the Spanish that is spoken to me out of the flying machines that I find it immediately comprehensible. I have no way of explaining this circumstance save to suggest that while in their externals the words may present themselves as Spanish, they belong in fact not to a local Spanish but to a Spanish of pure meanings such as might be dreamed of by the philosophers, and that what is communicated to me via the Spanish language, by mechanisms I cannot detect, so deeply embedded in me do they lie, is therefore pure meaning. This is my guess, my humble guess. The words are Spanish but they are tied to universal meanings. If I do not believe this then I must believe either that my witness is unreliable, which while it may disturb a third party does not concern either my voices or myself, the two parties who matter, since we seem to believe in each other; or that there is continuous miraculous intervention on my behalf in the form of translation, an explanation I choose not to accept until all others fail, preferring the less outrageous to the more outrageous.

242. How can I be deluded when I think so clearly?

243. The voices do not come directly to me out of the flying machines in any simple way. That is to say, men do not lean out of the flying machines and shout their words down to me.

Indeed, if the flying machines are large enough to hold men as I understand men, then they are only barely so. The flying machines, which look like narrow silver pencils with two pairs of rigid wings, a long pair in front and a short pair behind, are about six feet long, but fly hundreds of feet up in the air, higher than most birds, and consequently seem smaller than they are. They fly from north to south on the first and fourth days and from south to north on the second and fifth days, leaving the skies empty on the third, sixth, and seventh days. A cycle of seven days is one of the regularities I have discovered about the machines.

244. It is quite possible that there is only one machine which flies back and forth across the sky four times a week, rather than four machines or many machines. My mind is open on this point.

245. What flies across the sky is more like a machine than an insect because its drone is continuous and its flight perfectly regular. I call it a machine. It is possible that it is an insect. If so the joke is truly cruel.

246. The words I hear are not shouted down to me from the machines. Rather they seem to hang in suspension in the air, all those crystal Spanish vocables, and then to sift down as they grow colder, just as the dew does, and the frost in frost-time, and to reach my ears by night, or more often in the early morning just before dawn, and to seep into my understanding, like water.

247. I am not deluded; or if I am, my delusions are privileged. I could not make up such words as are spoken to me. They come from gods; or, if not, then from another world.

The words last night were: *When we dream that we are dreaming, the moment of awakening is at hand.* I ponder this text. I am sure it does not refer to my present state. I have never dreamt that

I am dreaming. I do not dream at all nowadays, but sleep a blissful passiveness waiting for the words to come to me, like a maiden waiting for the holy ghost. I am sure that I am real. This is my hand, bone and flesh, the same hand every day. I stamp my foot: this is the earth, as real to the core as I. Therefore the words must allude to a time yet to come. Perhaps they warn me that one day I will wake up feeling a trifle airier, a trifle more phantasmal than now, and, drawing the curtain and staring out across the veld for the millionth time, will find myself seeing each bush and tree, each stone and grain of sand, in its own halo of clarity, as if every atom of the universe were staring back at me. The rasp of the cicadas, so familiar as to be unheard, will begin to pulse in my ears, first with a soft pulse as though from a distant star, then louder until my skull reverberates with the shrilling, then softer, soft and steady, inside me. What will I say to myself then? That I have a fever, that my senses are for the time being deranged, that in a few days, if I rest, I will be my old self again? What incentive do fever microbes have to cross seven leagues of waterless scrub dotted with the pelts of long-dead merinos, assuming that fever is transmitted by microbes and microbes have wings? The reward of a single desiccated old maid? Surely the pickings are richer elsewhere. No, I fear that all I could say to myself would be: This cannot go on, I am losing myself, slumbertime is over, the moment of waking is at hand. And what shall I wake to? To that half-forgotten brown man lying tense and angry in my bed, his arm flung over his eyes? To the cold corridor outside my father's room, and the bedsprings' stealthy creak? To a rented room in a strange city where, on a stomachful of salt pork and potato salad, I have dreamed bad dreams all night? Or to some other predicament so bizarre as to be unimaginable?

248. The voices speak: *Lacking all external enemies and resistances, confined within an oppressive narrowness and regularity, man at last has no choice but to turn himself into an adventure.* They accuse me, if I understand them, of turning my life into a fiction, out of

boredom. They accuse me, however tactfully, of making myself more violent, more various, more racked with torment than I really am, as though I were reading myself like a book, and found the book dull, and put it aside and began to make myself up instead. That is how I understand their accusation. It is not in rebellion against true oppression that I have made my history, they say, but in reaction against the tedium of serving my father, ordering the maids, managing the household, sitting out the years; when I could find no enemy outside, when hordes of brown horsemen would not pour out of the hills waving their bows and ululating, I made an enemy out of myself, out of the peaceful, obedient self who wanted no more than to do her father's will and wax fat and full of days.

Are they gods and yet do not see, I ask myself, or is it I who am wilfully blind? Which is the more implausible, the story of my life as lived by me or the story of the good daughter humming the psalms as she bastes the Sunday roast in a Dutch kitchen in the dead centre of the stone desert? As for inventing enemies, the pitiful warrior in the hills was never as formidable as the enemy who walked in our shadow and said *Yes baas*. To the slave who would only say *Yes* my father could only say *No*, and I after him, and that was the start of all my woe. Therefore I protest. Some things are not visible from the skies. But how do I persuade my accusers? I have tried forming messages with stones, but stones are too unwieldy for the distinctions I need to make. And can I be sure they will even understand the words I use? If they are gods and omniscient, this is not a conclusion pointed to by their monolingualism. Can I even be sure they know about me? Perhaps they are quite ignorant of me. Perhaps I have been wrong all the time in thinking they speak to me. Perhaps their words are meant only for Spaniards, because unknown to me it has been decreed that Spaniards are the elect. Or perhaps the Spaniards do not live as far away as I had thought, but just over the hills. Think of that. Or perhaps I take their words too much to heart, perhaps they are meant neither for the Spaniards alone nor for me alone but for all of us, whoever we are, who understand Spanish, and we all stand accused of creating specious adventures, though this is harder to believe, not many people have as much time on their hands as I.

249. *The innocent victim can only know evil in the form of suffering. That which is not felt by the criminal is his crime. That which is not felt by the innocent victim is his own innocence.*

I am troubled here by my ignorance of the nuances of Spanish. I would be happier if these dicta were less sibylline. Do the voices here define crime and innocence or do they tell me of the modes in which victim and criminal experience the crime? If the former, do they assert that when evil is known as evil innocence is thereby destroyed? In that case I can enter the kingdom of the saved only as a farmgirl, never as a heroine of consciousness. Dare I say, Then I'll be damned? Will the voices cease to speak to me? If that happens I will truly be lost.

250. *It is the slave's consciousness that constitutes the master's certainty of his own truth. But the slave's consciousness is a dependent consciousness. So the master is not sure of the truth of his autonomy. His truth lies in an inessential consciousness and its inessential acts.*

These words refer to my father, to his brusqueness with the servants, his unnecessary harshness. But my father was harsh and domineering only because he could not bear to ask and be refused. All his commands were secret pleas – even I could see that. How then did the servants come to know that they could hurt him most essentially by obeying him most slavishly? Were they too instructed by the gods, through channels we were unaware of? Did my father grow harsher and harsher toward them simply to provoke them out of their slavishness? Would he have embraced a rebellious slave as a father embraces a prodigal son, though his next act might be to chastise him? Was my father crucified on the paradox the voices expound: that from people who bent like reeds to his whims he was asking, in his way, for an affirmation of his truth in and for himself?

And was it their provocation to reply *Yes baas* to his provocation, casting their eyes down, hiding their smiles, biding their time till he overreached himself? They must have known he had overreached himself when he moved Klein-Anna into the house. They must have known it before, when they saw his infatuation. Is that why Hendrik swallowed his pride? Did Hendrik not see in the seduction of Anna my father's last attempt to compel from the lips of a slave, albeit in the dead of night, words such as one free being addresses to another, words he could have had from me or from any of the perfumed widows of the region, but which coming from us would have been worthless? Or did Hendrik see it all clearly, and forgive nothing of it, but vow revenge? Is my banishment here Hendrik's revenge? Is it a sign of my innocence that I feel my banishment only as suffering, not as a crime against me? Where, unless compassion intervenes, does the round of vindictiveness end? *The voices stop too soon.* I am grateful for what they give me. Their words are golden. Neglected once, I am honoured for my years of solitude as few can have been. There is justice in the universe, I acknowledge. But the words from the sky raise more questions than they answer. I am gagging on a diet of universals. I will die before I get to the truth. I want the truth, certainly, but I want finality even more!

251. The stones. When first the machines began to fly overhead and speak to me I was eager to speak back. I would stand on the head of rock behind the house dressed for preference in white, in my patched old white nightdress, and signal with my arms and call out my responses, first in English, then later, when I began to see I was not understood, in Spanish. 'ES MI,' I shouted, 'VENE!' in a Spanish which I had to invent from first principles, by introspecting, as I went along.

252. Then it occurred to me that the beings in the machines might be flying in an ecstasy of self-absorption with their eyes fixed on the endless blue horizon, letting slip their messages

parenthetically, so to speak, to float down in their own good time. I therefore wondered whether I ought not to imitate the classic castaways and light a pyre to draw their attention. Labouring for three days I piled a mountain of dry brushwood. Then on the fourth day, as the first silver glint appeared in the northern sky, I set fire to my beacon and ran to my signalling post. Gigantic flames leapt into the sky. The air was filled with the crackling of thorns and the wheezes of expiring insects. 'ISOLADO!' I shouted against the roar, dancing about and waving a white handkerchief. Like a ghost the machine drifted above me. 'ES MI! VIDI!' I heard no answering voice.

253. But even if the being in the machine had spoken, I later realized, his voice would have been lost in the noise. Besides, I asked myself, what is there to make them think the fire is a signal? Might it not be simply a traveller's fire, or the straw bonfire of a contented agriculturist, or a veld-fire lit by a bolt of lightning, a mere phenomenon? I am, after all, not obviously a castaway, there is nothing to show that I cannot put one foot in front of the other till I reach the nearest aid post and ask for whatever it is I want, the comforts of civilization, say.

254. But perhaps, I then thought, I do them an injustice, perhaps they know very well I am a castaway, and smile among themselves, watching me dance about proclaiming my unique-ness while from horizon to horizon the world is dense with dancing folk signalling out of their private fires. Perhaps I am making a fool of myself, perhaps I will draw their attention and approval only when I give up my song and dance and go back to sweeping and polishing. Perhaps I am behaving like an ugly sister in a story in which only Cinderella is saved. Perhaps the millennium came and I, lacking a calendar, did not notice it, and now the prince is scouring the farthest reaches of the globe for his bride, and I, who have been hugging the parable so long to my heart, reading it as an allegory of my vindication, will find myself left behind with the clods while the blissful

pair fly off to a new life on the farther planets. What am I to do? I am lost both ways. Perhaps I should ponder further those words about the innocence of the innocent.

255. The stones. Having failed to make my shouts heard (but am I sure they did not hear me? Perhaps they heard me but found me uninteresting, or perhaps it is not their wont to acknowledge communications), I turned to writing. For a week, toiling from dawn to sunset, I trundled wheelbarrows full of stones across the veld until I had a pile of two hundred, smooth, round, the size of small pumpkins, in the space behind the house. These I painted, one by one, with whitewash left over from the old days (like a good castaway I find a use for every odd and end, one day I must make a list of things I have not used and then, as an exercise, find uses for them). Forming the stones into letters twelve feet high I began to spell out messages to my saviours: CINDRLA ES MI; and the next day: VENE AL TERRA; and: QUIERO UN AUTR; and again: SON ISOLADO.

256. After weeks of building messages, weeks filled with rolling stones about, repainting scratches, climbing up and down the steps to the loft to make sure my lines were straight, it struck me that what I was spelling out were not, strictly speaking, responses to the words that came to me from the sky, but importunities. Would one be tempted to visit a spot on earth, I asked myself, to which one was being so clamorously invited by so miserably lonely a creature, to say nothing of her age and ugliness? Would one not rather shun it like the plague? Therefore I put on my wide-brimmed hat on the days the machines flew and began to build messages that were quieter, more cryptic, in the style of their messages to me, and thus perhaps more alluring. POEMAS CREPUSCLRS, I announced on the first day, intending CREPUSCULARIAS but running short of stones. (Afterwards I brought in two dozen new stones in the wheelbarrow, there has never been any shortage of stones in

this part of the world, though what I am going to do with the painted stones when the machines stop flying I do not know, that is one anxiety I cannot dismiss, I may be driven to building a sepulchre outside the kitchen door, all ready to be crawled into when the great day comes, for I have not the heart to wheel them back into their native veld and disperse them, not after they have been brothers and sisters to each other so long, and participated in my messages.) SOMNOS DE LIBERTAD, I wrote on the second day; AMOR SIN TERROR on the fourth; DII SIN FUROR on the fifth; NOTTI DI AMITAD again on the first. Then I wrote a second poem, in six parts, responding to the various indictments of the voices: DESERTA MI OFRA – ELECTAS ELEMENTARIAS – DOMINE O SCLAVA – FEMM O FILIA MA SEMPRE HA DESIDER LA MEDIA ENTRE. The medium! Between! How I cursed my lot on the sixth of these days for denying me what of all things I needed most, a lexicon of the true Spanish language! To rack one's innate store for a mere conjunction when the word lay sleeping in a book somewhere! Why will no one speak to me in the true language of the heart? The medium, the median – that is what I wanted to be! Neither master nor slave, neither parent nor child, but the bridge between, so that in me the contraries should be reconciled!

257. Yet, ever charitable, I asked myself: What, after all, do my poems, even if understood, offer the sky-creatures? If they can build flying machines the attractions of a stone-moving, word-building intelligence must seem paltry. How can I *move* them? FEMM, I wrote, FEMM – AMOR POR TU. And, descending to ideographs, I spent all my stones on a sketch of a woman lying on her back, her figure fuller than mine, her legs parted, younger than myself too, this was no time for scrupulosity. How vulgar, I thought to myself, surveying the picture from the head of the steps, yet how necessary! And I cackled. How like the witch of fable I have grown. One might fear for the skymen that, drawn to earth by my lure, they will find themselves

metamorphosed into swine and reduced to eating slops. But perhaps they have felt this fear, and that is why they avoid me: perhaps on their travels over the rest of the world they pause in the treetops and converse with the groundsfolk, but when they pass over me soar high, dropping their cautionary messages.

258. I have also tried to ignore the nightly messages. One cannot pursue a hopeless infatuation, I have said to myself, without courting the fate of Narcissus. *A blind man dancing seems not to observe his period of mourning*, said the voices. Pooh! *It is a world of words that creates a world of things*. Pah!

259. Then last night the voice would not be stilled, but spoke on and on, no longer in tight little epigrams but in flowing periods, such that I wondered whether it were not a new god speaking, riding over my protesting clamour. 'Leave me, I want to sleep!' I shouted, drumming my heels. *It is in order that we shall not fall victim to the assassin*, said the voice, *that we consent to die if we ourselves turn assassin. Every man born in slavery is born for slavery. The slave loses everything in his chains, even the desire to escape from them. God loves no one*, it went on, *and hates no one, for God is free from passions and feels no pleasure or pain. Therefore one who loves God cannot endeavour to bring it about that God should love him in return; for, in desiring this, he would desire that God should not be God. God is hidden, and every religion that does not affirm that God is hidden is not true.* 'Go away,' I shouted, 'Spanish filth!' *Desire is a question that has no answer*, went on the voice – I know now for sure that they do not hear me – *The feeling of solitude is a longing for a place. That place is the centre of the world, the navel of the universe. Less than all cannot satisfy man. Those who restrain desire do so because theirs is weak enough to be restrained. When God accomplishes through the wicked what he has decreed in his secret counsels, the wicked are not thereby excusable. Those whom God leaves out of his election he is also reproving, and for no other reason than that he wills to exclude them.*

260. All day I have gone around with these words dinning in my ears, nagged by their air of significance, irritated by their lack of coherence. What assassin can be said to threaten me? How can one possibly consent to die? The flesh loves itself and cannot consent in its extinction. If I were truly a slave resigned to my chains would I not have learned the word *Yes* long ago? Yet where in my speech can *Yes* be pointed to? If my speech is not rebellious from beginning to end, what is it? As for the absence of God from the stone desert, there is nothing I can be told about this subject that I do not know. Everything is permitted here. Nothing is punished. Everything is forgotten in perpetuity. God has forgotten us and we have forgotten God. There is no love from us toward God nor any wish that God should turn his mind to us. The flow has ceased. We are the castaways of God as we are the castaways of history. *That* is the origin of our feeling of solitude. I for one do not wish to be at the centre of the world, I wish only to be at home in the world as the merest beast is at home. Much, much less than all would satisfy me: to begin with, a life unmediated by words: these stones, these bushes, this sky experienced and known without question; and a quiet return to the dust. Surely that is not too much. Are not all these dicta from above blind to the source of our disease, which is that we have no one to speak with, that our desires stream out of us chaotically, without aim, without response, like our words, whoever *we* may be, perhaps I should speak only for myself?

261. But I have other cares besides quarrelling with my voices. Sometimes when the weather is fine, as it is today, sunny but not too warm, I carry my father out of his room and seat him on the stoep, propped up with cushions in his old armchair, so that he can once again face out over the old acres, which he no longer sees, and be exposed to the birdsong, which he no longer hears. He sees and hears nothing, for all I know he tastes and smells nothing, and who can imagine what the touch of my skin on his is like? For he has retreated far, far into himself.

In the very chambers of his heart he crouches, wrapped in the pulsing of his faint blood, the far-off hiss of his breath. Of me he knows nothing. I pick him up without difficulty, a mannikin of dry bones held together by cobwebs, so neat that I could fold him up and pack him away in a suitcase.

262. I sit on the stoep by my father's side watching the world go by, the birds busy again with their nest-building, the breeze cool on my cheeks and perhaps on his too. 'Do you remember,' I say, 'how we used to go to the seaside, in the old days? How we packed a basket full of sandwiches and fruit and drove to the station in the trap and caught the evening train? How we slept on the train, rocked by the song of the wheels, waking drowsily at the water-stops, hearing the trainmen murmur far away, sleeping again; and how the next day we arrived at the seaside and went down to the beach and took off our shoes and paddled, you holding my hands and lifting me over the waves? Do you remember the hermit crab that pinched my toe, and how I cried and cried, and how you pulled faces to comfort me? Do you remember the boarding-house we stayed in? How tasteless the food was, and how one evening you pushed your plate aside and announced that you would not eat offal and stood up and left the dining-room?; and how I pushed my plate aside and followed you? And do you remember how happy the dogs were to see us back? There was one time when old Jakob forgot to feed them, and you swore terribly and took away his meat ration for a week. Do you remember Jakob and Hendrik and Ou-Anna and Klein-Anna? Do you remember that son of Ou-Anna's who was killed in an accident and brought back to the farm to be buried, and how Ou-Anna wanted to throw herself into the grave?

'Do you remember the years of the great drought, when the sheep had all to be sold because there was no grazing within two hundred miles, and how we had to struggle to build the farm up again? Do you remember the great old mulberry tree that stood on the other side of the chicken-run, and how one summer the trunk cracked down the middle under the weight of all the fruit? Do you remember how the earth around it would be stained purple with the juice of fallen berries? Do you remember the lovers' bench we used to have under the sering-tree, where you could sit all afternoon listening to the hum of the carpenter bees? Do you remember Vlek, who was such a good sheepdog that she and Jakob alone could drive a whole flock past you at the counting-post? Do you remember how Vlek grew old and sickly and could not hold down her food, and how there was no one to shoot her but you, and how you went for a walk afterwards because you did not want anyone to see you cry? Do you remember,' I say, 'those beautiful speckled hens we used to have, and the bantam cock with the five wives who used to roost in the trees? Do you remember them all?'

263. My father sits, if you can call it sitting, in his old leather armchair with the cool breeze on his skin. His eyes are sightless, two glassy blue walls rimmed with pink. He hears nothing but what goes on inside him, unless I am mistaken all this time and he hears all my chatter but chooses to ignore it. He has had his outing for the day; it is time to carry him in so that he can rest.

264. I lay my father out on his bed, unbutton his nightshirt, and unpin his napkin. Sometimes it is spotless; but today there is the faintest of stains, proving that somewhere inside him juices still dribble, muscles still execute their faint peristalses. I drop the old napkin in the bucket and pin on a new one.

265. I feed my father his broth and weak tea. Then I press my lips to his forehead and fold him away for the night. Once upon a time I used to think that I would be the last one to die. But now I think that for some days after my death he will still lie here breathing, waiting for his nourishment.

266. For the present, however, it appears that nothing is going to happen, that I may have long to wait before it is time to creep into my mausoleum and pull the door shut behind me, always assuming that I can find a pair of hinges in the loft, and drift into a sleep in which there are finally no voices teasing or berating me. At moments like the present, filled with lugubrious thoughts, one is tempted to add up one's reckoning, tie up the loose ends. Will I find the courage to die a crazy old queen in the middle of nowhere, unexplained by and inexplicable to the archaeologists, her tomb full of *naif* whitewash paintings of sky-gods; or am I going to yield to the spectre of reason and explain myself to myself in the only kind of confession we protestants know? To die an enigma with a full soul or to die emptied of my secrets, that is how I picturesquely put the question to myself. For instance: Have I ever fully explained to myself why I do not run away from the farm and die in civilization in one of the asylums I am sure must abound there, with picture-books at my bedside and a stack of empty coffins in the basement and a trained nurse to put the obol on my tongue? Have I ever explained or even understood what I have been doing here in a district outside the law, where the bar against incest is often down, where we pass our days in savage torpor – I who plainly had the makings of a clever girl who might have atoned for physical shortcomings with ten nimble fingers on the pianoforte keys and an album full of sonnets, who might have made a good wife, industrious, frugal, self-sacrificing, faithful, and even on occasion passionate? What have I been doing on this barbarous frontier? I have no doubt, since these are not idle questions, that somewhere there is a whole literature waiting to answer them for me. Unfortunately I am not acquainted with it; and besides, I have always felt easier spinning my answers out of my own bowels. There are poems, I am sure, about the heart that aches for Verlore Vlakte, about the melancholy of the sunset over the koppies, the sheep beginning to huddle against the first evening chill, the faraway boom of the windmill, the first chirrup of the first cricket, the last twitterings of the

birds in the thorn-trees, the stones of the farmhouse wall still holding the sun's warmth, the kitchen lamp glowing steady. They are poems I could write myself. It takes generations of life in the cities to drive that nostalgia for country ways from the heart. I will never live it down, nor do I want to. I am corrupted to the bone with the beauty of this forsaken world. If the truth be told, I never wanted to fly away with the sky-gods. My hope was always that they would descend and live with me here in paradise, making up with their ambrosial breath for all that I lost when the ghostly brown figures of the last people I knew crept away from me in the night. I have never felt myself to be another man's creature (here they come, how sweet the closing plangencies), I have uttered my life in my own voice throughout (what a consolation that is), I have chosen at every moment my own destiny, which is to die here in the petrified garden, behind locked gates, near my father's bones, in a space echoing with hymns I could have written but did not because (I thought) it was too easy.

J. M. Coetzee

DUSKLANDS

'Coetzee's vision goes to the nerve centre of being'
Nadine Gordimer

A specialist in psychological warfare is driven to breakdown and madness by the stresses of a project of macabre ingenuity to win the war in Vietnam. A megalomaniac Boer frontiersman wreaks hideous vengeance on a Hottentot tribe for undermining the 'natural' order of his universe with their anarchic rival order, mocking him and subjecting him to the humiliations of his own all too palpable flesh. Both the 18th century Jacobus Coetzee and the 20th century Eugene Dawn are in the business of pushing back the frontiers of knowledge and are dealers in death who denounce their own humanity and spurn their feelings of guilt. With immense power and economy in these two narratives, Coetzee has crystallized in their absurdity and horror, the extremes of scientific evangelism and heroic exploration.

'It's unflinching sense of loss, its claustrophobic acknowledgement of the unwilling interdependence of master and slave, and its subtle prose-style, make it an extraordinary achievement'
Guardian

VINTAGE

J. M. Coetzee

LIFE & TIMES OF MICHAEL K

'An astonishing book: lucid, graphic, sensitive…it will go on haunting me'
Observer

In South Africa, whose civil administration is collapsing under the pressure of years of civil strife, an obscure young gardener named Michael K decides to take his mother on a long march away from the guns towards a new life in the abandoned countryside. Everywhere he goes, however, the war follows him. Tracked down and locked up as a collaborator with the rural guerrillas, he embarks on a fast that angers, baffles, and finally awes his captors. The story of Michael K is the story of a man caught up in a war beyond his understanding, but determined to live his life, however minimally, on his own terms. J. M. Coetzee has produced a masterpiece which has the astonishing power to make the wilderness bloom.

'It strikes deep inside the heart…The story is clean, clear, straight, the work of a mature imagination at full power… here is a book that will be celebrated for a long time'
Mail on Sunday

VINTAGE

BY J.M. COETZEE
ALSO AVAILABLE IN VINTAGE

☐ Boyhood	009 926827 2	£6.99
☐ Disgrace	009 928952 0	£6.99
☐ Dusklands	009 926833 7	£5.99
☐ Life and Times of Michael K.	009 926834 5	£6.99
☐ The Master of Petersburg	0749 3963 2 6	£6.99
☐ Stranger Shores	009 942262 X	£8.99
☐ Waiting for the Barbarians	0749 3942 0 X	£6.99
☐ Youth	009 943362 1	£6.99

FREE POST AND PACKING
Overseas customers allow £2.00 per paperback

BY PHONE: 01624 677237

BY POST: Random House Books
C/o Bookpost, PO Box 29, Douglas
Isle of Man, IM99 1BQ

BY FAX: 01624 670923

BY EMAIL: bookshop@enterprise.net

Cheques (payable to Bookpost) and credit cards accepted

Prices and availability subject to change without notice.
Allow 28 days for delivery.
When placing your order, please mention if you do not wish to receive
any additional information.

www.randomhouse.co.uk/vintage